Also by Pete Kearney

RING SONGS

HITCHIN TO SEA LEVEL

STORY AVENUE

COVER DESIGN: LAWRENCE BUFFA

McMurdo

A Vietnam Diary

September 1970-71

Pete Kearney

McMurdo is a retelling of the diary I kept in Antarctica during the Vietnam War. Aside from asides and free associations these are the events that happened on the dates they happened.

I had a girl at McMurdo. Her family didn't approve of me; I wasn't a penguin. If you spend a year on the ice, people will gift you with penguin knickknacks for the rest of your life. Take my word for it -my home is overrun with porcelain Adélies.

I've read firsthand accounts of the Vietnam War and can assure my reader that mine contains no weapons specifications, battle maps or a guy named Tex. I served as far behind the fighting as you can get and still be in the same military.

I'm a young sailor among sailors supporting scientific research in Antarctica. Yippee! –we're not in Vietnam. We don't kill people or burn villages. We flaunt regulations in a climate that makes it easy to risk censure. What are they going to do – make us winter over? We are the winter over party and everything we do is influenced by the fact that when the summer people leave, we stay. If you're serving thirteen months, you bid the boys of summer goodbye at sunset. R&R means rack and read down here. Our dress blues are in storage. We're having a yearlong pajama party in service greens. You don't have to shave. Mail call ends when the sun don't shine.

Columbus Day, Oct 12, 1970

I land at the new world. Kees and I sit shoulder to shoulder for eight hours. We're in coach on a cargo plane. Backs against the bulkhead, we put our feet up on netted pallets. It's too loud to talk and everyone near us is sleeping. We land with a thud, as if the pilot missed a cellar step.

Four days earlier a VX6 plane took a spill at Willie Field. The landing tore a wing off. We taxi past her on tip toe. Her nose is pressed to the ice runway and her good wing signals like a drunk, at last call. The guys onboard that flight tell this war story.

Aboard the crashing aircraft is a Second Class Ships Serviceman Will Schuler. He's 6"3" and 280lbs less a meatball hero. From the sudden impact of impact, Schuler rose from his seat without unbuckling. He took the seatbelt housing off its anchor and deplaned wearing the harness like a parade Marshall. I wasn't there. I didn't see it. If its bullshit, there's a crew of guys swearing to it. Everyone onboard owns that war story.

10/13.The sun lights the day and the sun lights the night. There's no place near here like here. McMurdo is an ice hub. You overnight with us on your way to the outlying stations. We even have an airport shuttle. South of us is a white world. Our base is a brownie square dusted with fine snow and volcanic ash, the last stop for a stagecoach. The sun sits still as an accent over a letter in a foreign word.

A Quonset hut is a soup can cut top to bottom. Set one half on its side and enlarge it to the size of an equipment barn and you've described the firehouse/movie theater. It's my 21st birthday when I first sign the log.

Bug juice and powdered eggs start a McMurdo busy day. There are big projects to accomplish while the sun is up. Twenty-seven separate departments come ashore in the same week. The men we replace trot off the field an exhausted defense.

I'm assigned to mess cook. I know my firehouse crew; we've spent the summer in Rhode Island. Now I'm in a mix of guys drawn from a mix of departments at the base. I'm banding skids of supplies; I know how to skate. It's my second year in the Navy.

At the firehouse, our movie feature is The Viking Queen. Second Class Tom Conrad is our projectionist. When he's ready to start he yells "Movie" in a crowded firehouse.

10/14. Second day at mess cooking, I'm in the chow hall busing tables in kitchen whites. I have a paper Boy Scout cap tipped back on my head. I'm doing a twelve hour shift with breaks between meals.

Our winter-over party is here to hold post after dark. The summer crews undertake capital improvements in a town that sleeps with the lights on. In February the summer-overs will sparrow back to Christchurch. During their season, everything is fixed whether it needs it or not. Our command is charged with maximizing conditions for next year's party. It is understood that the guys we relieved left everything screwed up. An isolated unit on a nondescript hillside, we play no part in the war.

10/15. A number of men here have done a tour in Nam. Their war stories make great sea stories. Comparing assignments is absurd. Vietnam has pot, alcohol and pussy. McMurdo has pot and alcohol. We don't have guns. The way you get killed here is to fall into an ice crevasse or step in front of a front loader. Fatal accidents are rare. We serve on a continent without a recorded homicide – a slice of the American military not involved with imposing its will overseas.

While bussing tables I overhear a Seabee telling his friend that Mayor Daley ordered the Kent State shootings.

Antarctica is a lonely continent where everyone lives in close quarters. In the summer, McMurdo has 600 men crammed into a base no bigger than the poor side of town. Officers and Chiefs get their own rooms; the rest of us have three or more roommates. There is no unused living space during the summer. You want to be alone, go outside.

Jack and Andy come by and we go down to the harbor to smoke two joints. My gear has yet to catch up with me. I've carried pot in my socks.

10/16. As an E-2 storekeeper striker assigned to the firehouse, I am the lowest enlisted man in the winter-over contingent. I know why I'm here. Every shit detail including the shit detail is on my to-do-do list. I'm not put off by it. I have a mission-avoid the war.

We get our first alarm at 0400. The firehouse has a fire pole that we slide down to man our assigned trucks and fight a false alarm. When we get back to the house I stay up. After work I go to John's room and walk in on a wake. Les has lost all his dope. Whoever found it turned it over to Rittenhour, the hard ass Bosin Chief. My supply of grass and pills becomes more significant. Tonight's movie is <u>The Tiger Makes Out.</u>

10/17. All my gear is in a black footlocker and a sea bag. Kees gave me his weight allowance, which enabled me to pack a stack of albums. At Willie Field, my stuff goes missing. I'm living with the clothes on my back and a toothbrush bummed from John. On a break between meals, I find my stuff dumped outside the firehouse. Overcome with the thrill of reuniting with my gear, I drag my footlocker upstairs and stow it under my rack. Darden chews my ass for leaving scuff marks on the deck.

10/18. First Sunday in town breakfast runs into lunch. People have been busting ass - the men we relieved have left in a scrum. New faces arrive at every meal. They console themselves if they're only staying for the summer.

Dinner is turkey and we have a full house. There's drinking and high spirits. I'm working the floor with a young black guy, Robby Robinson.

"I roll from the double O-Oberlin, Ohio," he says as if asked.

Robbie and I shoot pool at the firehouse. Stick and Nealey come in drunk and challenge us. I tell Nealey to piss off and he wants to fight. He calls Robbie "black boy" and I have to stop Robbie from swinging the bridge at him. Robbie is smaller than me and I'm not big. We are chip on the shoulder featherweights ready to fight if the other is threatened. An alarm sounds and we run to our trucks. Stick puts his vehicle up against the side of the firehouse.

10/19. Andy comes to town with two dudes from Willie Field. We go out into the daylight night and smoke joints. Andy and I are winter-over. The summer guys want to party hard but I'm conserving my resources. Those who smoke know who has how much weed. Trades are proposed and dismissed. Each no dawn day reveals reduced inventory. Over-indulge at your own risk; don't forget you're staying the winter.

10/20. Robbie and I climb up to the galley overhead storage area and sleep on bags of flour. We get breaks on both sides of lunch but can't secure till Chief Smithy sniffs the sheets. The firehouse is standing room only as Homer premiers his XXX movie. Our Officer Mr. Pruitt is on site. A peeping Tom watches a woman undress-you know the rest. Stick is drunk again and when an alarm rings in the laundry he crashes his truck into Bldg 155 and cracks the windshield.

10/21. Kees sees me in the mess hall. The Chief has banned all drinking at the firehouse. Two accidents during our first week here –no shit- the Chief should be pissed. We wonder if Stick will lose a stripe. He's a second class Damage Controlman. When sober, he is more capable than the rest of us combined.

Over in Nam, there's a Chinese menu of mood elevators. Down here its liquor, smoke and pills while living in close quarters with lifers. You can get away with being stoned but psychedelics are risky. There is a chance you might get spooky and spark some science fiction resulting in a base wide inspection.

Back at the firehouse, we get our first mail. My sister Mary Lou writes to say she has joined the Army. My cousin Danny writes to say he hasn't.

Mail Call 10/20/70... My cousin Danny

Pete

How are you guy? Long time no hear! If you're still with me at this point I'll keep writing. Wake up!!!

I guess winter is lots of fun down there. Getting a lot of skiing in? Sorry I haven't written in these past months but I don't feel so bad cause you didn't either.

Let me now take you on a magical mystery tour of my life these past months –zzzzz- wasn't that great?

Well your smart junior exec has been laid off of work again for a little over two months. Terrific!! I still haven't gotten a job –what a bum! I'm presently on unemployment.

Also shortly after I lost my job I lost my car. It was totaled out on the Belt Parkway one night. I just bought another car though, pray for protection! I bought a 66 Ford convertible – classy!

I'm also doing fairly well in school (so far). I really wonder why I go to the most expensive school on Long Island for bullshit. Tuition just went up to $72 per credit. Ridiculous! Loans, loans and more loans.

Everyone in the family is doing OK as far as I know. How are you doing? Get rid of the frost bite on your pecker?

The old lady (Rose) is doing OK. She got laid off (pun) from her job about three weeks ago. No shit! A cop kicked her off her corner and she hasn't found a good replacement. (Don't you ever repeat that or I'll piss on you.)

No kidding, she did lose her job but she found another within a couple of weeks. I haven't been doing much else besides going to school. Oh yeah I'm going to summer school to catch up on some credits. What a drag!

I've seen your friend and mine Pat Hughes. He said about a month and a half ago he wrote you a letter but that you didn't return it. Bad Boy! The latest from Bob Huckemeyer is that he may be going in the service, (I think the Navy). No shit. What an abortion that will be!

I also have to tell you that Harry Strickrod has beat the draft. He went for a physical all drugged up. Not bad if you can do it.

I haven't seen or heard anything about your family. Tell me how your brother Artie is doing and your sister Mary Lou. Oh yes guess what I did? Can't? I figured. Well I bought a ten speed racing bike (not a motorcycle dummy). I bought it so I could use it until I got a car. It's pretty good though, I enjoy doing it.

Tell me what you've been doing these past months when you write back. You will write back!! Have you gone to New Zealand? Any time off? When you going home from your hole in the earth? When are you finally gonna get out of the service? What do you have? Another two years?

I guess I'm gonna say adios before I make this letter a complete abortion. So be good, keep way from the sweeties down there.

Danny

Oh yeah, you still going with Kathy? I haven't seen her since you left. How's she doing? Fill me in.

10/21. Fang and Mike, two radiomen stoners arrive from Willie Field. We've been getting high in D'Ville all summer and now we're looking at each other in McMurdo. Robby and I drop THC with Andy and Jack.

We drift down to the ice shelf and watch the sun refuse to set. Our ambition is to use psychedelics to enhance our appreciation of our circumstances. The Royal Society Range owns the horizon. The whiteness between it and us covers the Ross Sea with a hospital sheet. When tripping you want to be around people you trust. Andy and Jack are from the strip. Robbie and I are townies. Everyone is obliged to behave within reason. You shouldn't spoil the party with any loss of cool.

10/22. I get word that Second Class Darden is taking over my rack. John and I buy record players from the ships store. I leave mine in John's room because I'm without a bed. I wind up sleeping at Quonset Hut 22 with a scullery crew of Seabees. Seabees are landlocked construction battalions set aside from the black shoe navy. This team of good ole boys is doing 30 days of dishwashing. I am regular Navy with a Yankee accent. I work out on the floor busing tables.

"You hang out with that nigger kid." It's the only thing they say to me the night I move in.

10/23. I report to the galley at 0530. The Chief sends me back to Hut 22 to wake the Seabees but I decide I've misunderstood. I don't respond with an actual "Aye aye". Let those pricks get written up; I'm not their alarm clock. At night, Robby and I play pool against two lifer cooks named Bell and Barnes. While I'm stretching across the table to line up a shot, Barnes whispers in my ear.

"Kearney, I'm gonna fuck you."

Jeez, I've been here a week and a day and I'm already the cabin boy. We start playing eight ball for money and when the night ends, Bell gives me $13.50. Barnes won't pay Robby.

"I'm not giving money to a nigger."

I split my winnings with Robby. We hear that Barnes is being transferred to Palmer station.

Homer has us plant dry chemical fire extinguishers in a snow bank outside the firehouse to test their resistance to the cold. Kees adds a sign that reads Ansul Garden. This type of detail fills my diary. I recap every day with a one-page letter, self-addressed.

10/24. The Chief sends me back to Hut 22 to wake the Seabees. He doesn't ask me why I ignored him yesterday.

"Wake up, Pukes!" I slam their door and run back to the galley.

In the lull between breakfast and lunch, I hear the Seabee dishwashers muttering when I come near. I'm feeding dirty dishes onto a conveyor through a window in the wall. When I step into their work area a kid called Chicken Man starts bracing me. A couple of his mates join him and I'm pressed against the dishwasher. A guy named Ghetto cuffs me on the back of my head. "I don't like being called puke".

I sucker punch Ghetto with no effect. We slip down on the wet floor of the scullery - him on top. The fall breaks my fall. My breath leaves me as he pulls a metal meal tray off the sink and slices open my eyebrow. The fight is broken up and I go the dispensary and get three stitches. The Corpsmen seem thrilled with a chance to suture. I'm walking around with heightened vital signs. Pushing two chairs together in the firehouse movie room I sleep as well as I can.

10/25. After breakfast, Robby complains of a toothache and comes back from the dispensary with a handful of pills that we divide and consume. The scullery crew smirks at my bandaged eye. I get some lame catcalls. Ghetto comes by to gloat. He's carrying around an acoustic guitar. Great- I've had my ass kicked by a singer-songwriter. I have to be ready to fight again or I invite further abuse. I don't want to fight but I have no choice. I've been drafted. I sit through the movie The Student Prince, don't ask me how. I'm resolved to working with guys who want to kill me.

10/26. Sixty-six days left on the calendar year; I'm sleeping on waiting room furniture. I have stitches in my eyebrow and spend my days wiping down tables in the mess. The Chief insists that the condiment bottles on each table line up precise as chorus girls. He stands at the galley door with one eye closed and directs their alignment. The Navy relies on the power of objects suitably arranged so that in darkness or smoke you know exactly where your hot sauce is. In Vietnam, they conduct body counts. We know that until the sun goes down and then returns, we're not going anywhere near gunfire.

I lose Robby as a partner; he is promoted to assistant cook and stays in the galley. I work the floor with a slender white kid named Joe Farmer who I call Farmer Joe. Tonight kicks off Gedunk hours; you can eat a hamburger or a hotdog with a soda or beer starting at 2200. Lt. Eastlick plays guitar.

McMurdo is a lonely little mining town crammed with Seabees, regular Navy and a squad of civilian scientists. Building 155 is mother ship to Quonset huts, sheds and garages. It's where most everybody eats and sleeps. On the shoulder of Observation Mountain, the nuclear power plant oversees town. When we're living on nuclear power our engineering officer wears a red belt. It's a small world made smaller if you have to worry about being mugged by Seabees.

The firehouse head is a single-seat affair posed over a 55-gallon drum cut in half and lined with a plastic bag. Opening the base, pulling out the can, removing the full bag and dragging it to the dump is "honey bagging" – a responsibility assigned to the lowest enlisted man. Hauling shit has advantages. No one wants to take your job away. The cold mutes the smell and you can kill an hour doing it. Downwind from town the dump burns waste materials while overseen by the McMurdo fire department. Human waste doesn't decompose at this latitude.

10/27. Two weeks after touchdown, I'm still sleeping on a love seat in the firehouse movie theatre. After mess cooking I go to John's room. A couple of his neighbors come in high on mescaline. It is 1970 and we're in the United States Navy. In a culture tolerant of alcohol abuse, some of us elect to get drunk on pills. Hanging out with trippers is like being sober around drunks who don't throw up. The pills won't slur your voice or make you belligerent. You're apt to think they make you profound. The firehouse movie is We Joined the Navy

10/28. There is tension at the mess hall. The Seabees want a piece of me. They think I sneak punched Ghetto knowing a fight wouldn't last but a minute. What did he think I was going to do, shake his hand? This giraffe- looking dude Byrnelsen tries to slip a melting ice cream bar into the side pocket of my jacket. High school stuff, but the Seabees are bored to death with dishwashing.

10/29. We find out Farmer Joe is being assigned to Byrd so we all drop THC at a going away party. Mac, John and I are well underway when Robbie and Farmer join us. We go outside and walk down to the ice field. McMurdo is dirt roads of volcanic dust. The town is a jumble of once green buildings and huts the color of rusted cans. There's equipment lying around and Conex boxes that no one claims. You come down to the ice shelf if you want to see white.

10/30. I'm still high the next day. Griffith is transferred out of the firehouse so that opens up a rack for me. I stuff a locker and set up my stereo. Now I'm sleeping on Government Issue. Wilson is written up for being drunk. Kilpatrick comes to the galley and pukes. Its payday, I draw $69 from disbursement.

10/31. Halloween means partying and the juicers are blasting country music at the Chief's club across the street. Along with pot and pills, I brought a collection of albums to the ice. This gives me a leg up at being a DJ at the base radio station WASA. No one is sure our programs have listeners but I'm enthusiastic about getting on the air.

On our way down from Davisville, Rhode Island, we stopped at Los Angeles, Honolulu, Pago Pago and Christchurch. All the way down I'm reading Endurance – the story of Ernest Shackleton's Antarctic adventures. After two weeks here, it's hard to relate. I eat three meals a day and a midnight snack, sleep on a soft rack and watch a movie every night. I'm not sucking on seal blubber in a shack with ZZ Top.

The polar exploration I undertake involves expeditions into my own mind. Mescaline, THC, hash and pot are the sled dogs to mind expansion. It's a topic, which intrigues the members of my book club. It supposes to be more than just getting high but getting high is the starting line. Adam and Eve got busted for ingesting apple in hope to be more like God. They did it in a much warmer time zone. The idea that I can access spirituality by using street pills seems absurd except it works. I romantically believe I've moved from unaware to more aware about the folly of war. My mates and I dip our toes into hallucinogenic magic. We consider it a spiritual exercise when done alone or in the company of one other. It's not always partying. There is time for reflection here. We debate whether acid saved or destroyed the Beatles.

I know why I'm here and it has to do with the war. I would go if I was sent.   I'm regular Navy – I'm not going to wind up in the bush. Everyone over there plays at least a supporting role. Just because you're not in the shit doesn't mean your hands are clean.

Allow me this observation – the supernatural occurs every day in a million miniscule ways. I can't explain why another guy has to die while I eat mid-rats. The universe is not concerned with my lack of understanding. I should not question my own dumb luck.

It's not that cold because the sun is up all day. No one starves at a Navy base. If it wasn't for the Dukes of Hazard looking to gang bang me, this would be ice-skating duty. When there's nothing else to do I play records.

11/1. I've been here less than a month but it seems longer. There is bingo in the chow hall at night. Early for that kind of thing, isn't it? Sleep is a concern for everyone. The firehouse movie is A Summer Place.

11/2. Andy's birthday, we present him with a cherry pie. A few of us meet in Jack's room and drop THC. Andy is tall, gaunt and incapable of growing a beard. His straight blonde hair and smooth features suggest a movie star bad boy. We are so buzzed that we get paranoid our Chief will read our faces. Hiding out at the radio station doesn't work. We're a disruption that Second Class Wilson can't handle - he kicks us out. Walking around town in 2300 daylight, the only men we meet are other intoxicated insomniacs. You can't sleep while on pills. Along with others out of their racks, we converge in the mess hall - five hours early for breakfast.

With the 24 hour sun, you get a condition called big eye or red eye. Your eyes bulge and feel sandy. You can't sleep despite being exhausted. Beer and booze are dirt-cheap sleeping pills. If you don't drink it's your own fault. I carried down a supply of Visine- to disguise being stoned. Now I see everyone around me is red-eyed.

11/3. I write to my brother Tom. Intending to be light I write the opposite. Tom is a year older than me, and not going to Vietnam. One of the 100,000 hippies who crashed DC, he spent a night in lock-up with tear gas tears in his eyes. My oldest brother Artie and my younger sister Mary Lou are both Army. Tom is the one with the war story. My parents have invited him to leave home.

11/4. Robby gets orders for Beardmore Station. We eat at a firehouse barbeque. It is one of the million buddy bonds made in the ice floe of military service.

Robbie is on a summer tour. He'll pass through town on his way home. Talking about sex he says, "The worst I had was good."

Our sleeping quarters on the second deck of the firehouse feature three racks tucked beneath the curving alcove created by our roof. Opposite them are three built in bunks at mid-ship. At the bottom of the room is a free standing rack that I call home. The room sleeps seven and six snore. I listen. I have a record player and impose my taste on my roommates. Complaints are voiced, I have no clue I'm pissing people off.

11/6/70 Mail Call ...My sister Susie

Dear Peter,

HI! Since none of us, except Mom & Dad have gotten a letter from you recently, we figured you must have forgotten or something (hint hint).

Not much has been happening around here. My big job lasted exactly one week when I was (as you say in

America) fired. (O.K. Stop laughing). I didn't make enough sales – only 2 for the week. I really was not right for the job. I felt really guilty trying to sell these stupid magazines to some really nice people. Half the time, they'd think it was a joke and hang up or start yelling at me or tell me they were going to call the cops –boy was it fun. It really got boring too –you had to sit in this ugly yellow office and keep calling and calling. It was really bad on Saturday, we had to start calling at 9AM. Most of the people were sleeping and got really mad when they had to get up to answer the phone. So the other day – last Monday – the guy from work called and said since I wasn't making enough sales they'd have to let me go – believe me, I wasn't exactly all broken up when I heard it. I was supposed to get paid $1.60 an hour but he paid me $1.75 instead so I got a $30 check in the mail – I can sure use it. I bought a sweater and today I have to buy pants.

As you already know, Billy came home Thursday night. He was slightly stoned. I didn't see him but all the kids said he was really good-looking.

Clare's big romance with Greg D. is cooling off. She doesn't like his short bells and white socks. (I'm only kidding-usually he wears blue socks with them).

In a recent letter to Mother you mentioned that when you get home I'll have the sorest pair of knees in Maria Regina. I wouldn't place any bets on that. Rene is aggravated at your insinuation that she's too grouchy to write a letter – so far she's written two and you haven't replied.

Yesterday in school, some stupid boy dropped a match in the boy's room garbage pail. We had the big fire drill (of course when I was supposed to be eating lunch). Black smoke was pouring out of the windows but in twenty minutes everything was okay.

On Wednesday we had our big Moratorium Day activities. First we had a debate with two speakers – a Jesuit priest who was against the war and a guy from

31

*the American Legion who was for the country. Dad
was really mad when I told him the Jesuit was
comparing our government with the government of
the Nazi Third Reich. Some girl got up and was really
mad – she goes "How could you ever compare that
maniac Nazi government with the democratic
government of today?" Everyone started clapping &
whistling for her and waving the American flag in the
air. That is – everyone except the few with the black
arm bands and peace signs. Then they showed two
movies "Why Vietnam?" and "No Vietnamese Ever
Called Me Nigger." Both of them stunk. After that they
had a conscientious objector which I missed. Daddy is
quite mad –he's writing a letter to the principle. He
didn't exactly like the day's program, especially the
Jesuit. Well I'd better go – you better write or you'll
have the sorest pair of knees in the Navy when you
get home.
Love Susie*

11/7. It is party night in Butch's room. Les, Joe, John and I take THC. We listen to music and bullshit about Davisville. We have spent this past summer driving around Rhode Island smoking joints and eating hamburgers. Butch is an Alpha male and talks about pussy as something disembodied from a female. It's a subject remote as astrophysics. He advises us to do our utmost to get pussy whenever possible. "We all answer to a higher power". He is practically asking us to take a blood oath. There are no girls here and none are expected so the Reverend Butch sermon seems hilarious. We are stoned enough to find anything anybody says funny. In reality going without sex is nothing new for most of us. I don't think anyone at the party is even married. Butch is a summer support, what does he have to cry about?

11/8. Sunday is a slack day. We don't report to the galley until 7am. I finish the book Another Country by James Baldwin during breaks between meals. The firehouse movie that night is Cool Hand Luke. We repeat the line "Taking it off here, Boss" whenever given a chance. The lifer Darden complains he can't sleep with all the bullshit going on so we move to the 155 galley where Britain, Chambers and a guy I don't know play guitars like a poor man's Beach Boys.

11/8/70 Mail Call ... Tom Z

Pete,

How's the weather? I'm going swimming tomorrow and I'll be thinking of you freezing your balls off down there. It's suppose to be in the high 90"s. What are the temperatures like down there?

My ship came back the 30th and I went over to it on the 31th. Boy does it suck, I had it better over in Nam. It's one big pile of shit. I really can't believe this is happening. I never did anything to anybody. Why me?

The CALIENTE should be taken out to sea and have the fuck blown out of it. Almost everything on the ship is busted and the things that work are falling apart. They're going to put the ship in the yard for five or six months and try to fix it. They'll never be able to fix it up, it's too far gone. It's just going to be a big waste of money but you know the navy.

While you're down on the ice do you get any R&R or do they keep you down there a full year? How are your fuck books going? You should have your own library by the time you leave. Too bad you won't be able to practice what you write while you're down there.

Well, I got to go, I have duty today and I have to empty the shit-cans. Take it easy and keep cool   -Z

11/9. John's birthday. He and I have been in each other's company almost every day for the past year. He has been my roommate, smoking partner, tripping partner and buddy from the buddy system. Barstow and I make him a birthday cake and bring it to his room after work. Butch suggests banana sledding. Using a Public Works truck, we drive to a crest on

Observation Hill where the slope drops as a dragon coaster. A dude named Ronnie wipes out after ten yards and his sled continues down the slope at the speed of an arrow. I go next and stay on all the way down avoiding a rocky outcropping that should have killed me. We all go back to base to put on warmer clothes. Back at the starting gate, I double up with Joe Jones. The sled throws me off but Jones is caught in the bindings and breaks his leg. He has to wait for the others to sled down before he gets dropped off at sick bay.

11/12. I have ten days left as a mess cook. The Seabee scullery crew does the best it can to bully me. A juice freak named Wilson calls me out and I manage to slip away without getting my head kicked in. I'm above schoolyard brawls; psychedelics have given me a glimpse of the bigger picture. If I wanted to fight, I would have gone to Vietnam.

Meanwhile in Southeast Asia, the United States has concluded its road tour into Cambodia. Congress imposed an eighteen-mile limit on the incursion and a check out time of July 30. The enemy marked its calendar while encamped 22 miles from the border. Our ARVNs displayed a talent for seizing abandoned supply depots. The fall of 1970 brings a plan to invade Laos, part of a whack-the-hippo approach to keeping busy. Intelligence reports describe heavily fortified enemy positions in inaccessible jungles. The brush is said to be ripe with anti–aircraft.

Mail Call. 11/12/70. My sister Susie.

Peter,

Hi, I hope everything is okay with you. Right now I'm in history class – the teacher has been reading an article for the last 20 minutes and I can't take it anymore! I'm really glad I was home Sat. night when you called even though I only heard you for a second – the connection was really bad. I don't know if you could hear us all say goodbye when you got off but that's what we screamed. Please try to write home more, I know you must be busy but Mom's going crazy, that one typed letter didn't tell us too much.

Saturday afternoon I went with Mom for an interview at Miss Skinner's Secretarial School and it was really good. They have all new electric typewriters, dicta phones etc. Half of it is a charm course – I know I can just skip over that but I think I'll brush up a little (alright stop laughing). If I do go there I'll have to have a car which is good. I'm taking Drivers Ed, next summer but I don't think I'll have enough money for a car for awhile. Right now I have $500 but I'm thinking of going to Germany and Austria at Easter and using it all on that. I'd really like to go on the trip but I want a car too. If a lot of my friends go, I'll forget about the car till I get back.

School isn't too bad. The first quarter ends this week and I think I'll do okay. If I fail anything this year, there goes the job. Mom and Dad say I'm out too much and that my marks better not go down but I'm not really worried. I'm glad my courses are pretty easy.

Work itself is great. The only bad thing is that we have to wear uniforms now and they have to be the ugliest things I've ever seen. Up till now we've just had to wear a white blouse, any skirt and a gold apron. First they got us these gross hats to wear. They're bright orange and they look like a nurses cap sort of. Now they have uniforms for us. Its black silky material, V neck, comes in at the waist and then balloons out at the hips besides being midi length. They're giving us a break though and letting us shorten them. I think I'll accidently cut it up while shortening it.

This past weekend was pretty bad. There's a kid from work (Jim) that I'm pretty good friends with. Last weekend he got two tickets for a Knicks game at the last minute from his friend. All the kids were working so he asked me to go (what a compliment huh). We went and I had a good time. I took it as just good friends but now I found out he took it differently. He's nice but I don't want to go out with him. Besides I like this kid Billy and we're sort of going out but Jim doesn't know it. Oh, such problems I'm sure you're interested. Just don't mention anything about it to Mom. She still is bothering me about Kevin. Well I'd better go. Please write home more often or at least try to take care of yourself.

Love Susie

P. S. Your picture came out really great. It makes you look much older and the colors are just right – I guess miracles do happen sometimes- only kidding of course.

11/13. We go on water hours. Everyone eats off paper plates with plastic utensils. If you're a dishwasher or a bus boy it's your Fourth of July. People bus their own tables so I float around like a maître-de on weed. On the way back to the firehouse, I trudge through a big league snowstorm. I can see birds out over the bay. I have letters from my brother John and my sisters Nancy and Shelia. I don't say a word when Laine yells at me to turn my record player down.

11/14/70 Mail Call... My Dad

Dear Peter,

Here goes my third attempt to cover your recent letter. Sorry that I ended yesterday's so abruptly but the last mail was going out of the office and I wanted to get it off. I hope that you receive them in sequence.

You make a valid point when you say that I'm disappointed that my children, or some of them, do not share my religious convictions but if you equate my religious convictions with mere mechanical forms ("spiritual refreshment every Sunday") rather than substance you do me an injustice. I adhere to the outward evidence of my faith because doing so is demonstrating that I am committed to it. Going to Mass on Sunday is a matter of pride – if I voluntarily belong to an organization, I follow the rules. If they change the rules on Sunday observance (it's being discussed) I could change as easily as I did when Friday abstinence was scrubbed. Yet when meatless Friday was the rule, I observed it regardless of where I

was or with whom I was. I have a great respect for my
Protestant friends and respect their beliefs as they
respect mine. It does cause me to wonder however if I
have wasted my time and effort trying to insure my
children a religious oriented education when they
found it so easy to forget.

Religion in general calls for an ethical belief. The
courts in this country have even raised non-religion to
the status of religion based on the principle that a
code of ethics does not necessarily require a belief in
God. The common denominator however is the code
of ethics - the belief that some things are right and
others wrong.

There is a large area of agreement in Western
religions on basic ethical values. Admittedly, I
subscribe to a very strict code – it is wrong to kill,
steal, lie, cheat, engage in extra martial sex etc. - you
know the list. A great many of my friends, Catholic,
Protestant, Jew, atheist or agnostic share some or all
of these values. It disappoints me when my sons do

not because as I tried to point out, it is an absolute rejection of the example I tried to give

My whole way of life depends on being unselfish. I do not put my interests first. Young people today talk an awful lot about love for their fellowman but too rarely, do they sacrifice their own comfort just to make someone's life a little more pleasant, especially if it is an older person involved. It may seem petty for a mother to ask her daughter to wear a skirt rather than shorts or jeans to an affair or ask her son to shave and wear a tie, so that she will be proud of them but really –is it such a great sacrifice for the kids involved to comply? Or does it equate to a mother footing the bill and doing the work so her daughter can have a party – a small effort when compared to the pleasure given someone else?

The trouble with religion today is that most organized religions in this country have fallen prey to the social problem syndrome. Young people turn to the mysticism of Oriental religions; yoga, drugs and the

occult in search of some deep spiritual meaning.
There's a spiritual meaning in Christianity, if one seeks
it. Religion should not be concerned with trying to
change social patterns as it eventually must serve as a
personal guide for people on both sides of an issue. If
religion can teach the individual to do only good the
widespread injustices have to disappear. The day that
my sons can say their religion is deeper than doing
what seems the easiest course to follow is the one I
wait for – to be continued. Love Dad.

11/14. In my kitchen whites and a paper hat, I steer my cart around the dining room watching people eat. If any of my crew is eating I'll sit with them for a few minutes with my head on a swivel looking for the Chief. During the breaks between meals, I read and try to appear invisible.

Kees returns from fire patrol excited about a shed with a giant UT spray-painted in orange on its door. It's Russ Peterman's USARP lab. Nothing makes a Texan as happy as meeting another Texan outside Texas.

Mail Call 11/14/70   Tom Z

Happy Birthday Salty, I would have bought you a card but I don't have a dime to my name. I lost my wallet in Long Beach with about $35 in it, along with my ID. What pisses me off is I wasn't even drunk. I didn't even have a drink the whole time I was there. I got back to the gate and went for my wallet to show my ID and it wasn't there. I was hoping some honest citizen of Long Beach would find it and return it but I guess some fucking sailor found it , took the money and threw the wallet away,

On the second of December were going from Long Beach to San Pedro and then on the 7th we're going out to sea for four days to clean tanks. I can hardly wait to crawl down into those tanks and get full of dirt and oil.

I haven't really been doing much lately. About two weeks ago I went into town and drank a pint of scotch in a movie theatre. I drank it straight and after we left the theatre I could hardly walk. The guy I was with only had a half-pint so he was sober enough to get us back to the ship.

How's the weather? Is it cold enough for you? I bet you miss the smog of New York. I guess you don't have to worry about having a white Christmas, do you? Right now it's raining in smoggy California.

Since we left Nam, they've had two typhoons and one tropical storm. I got a letter the other day from the second class I worked for over there. He said the place where I worked got tore up by the storms. This guy who wrote me is a second class who just went over there on Oct 12 and is getting out around the 30th of this month .He's getting over a ten month cut. I hope I get a nice big cut out of your Navy.

Do you get any R&R or anything while you're down there? If you stay down there a year straight you'll probably come back and ship over for some more bennies.

A friend of mine who is also a mess cook asked me to ask where you throw your garbage so here goes – Where do you throw your garbage?

How are your sex novels coming? You should have a whole series done by the time you leave.

Got to go - keep cool, dude... Z.

11/15. Butch drives us up to what we call Suicide Hill. The three of us are clinging to the sides of supersized forklift. John has given us each a half tab of THC. KP and I get face down on a banana sled. I'm in front and he's lying atop me. We are staring down a white slope so steep it seems to disappear. When we push off, the sled pops me under the chin. I see stars as we rocket downhill. After a free fall and a couple of bounces on the icy slope we curve into a snowdrift. Britain follows us solo. Butch drives the forklift down to pick us up. While waiting for Butch, a Chief out for a walk starts chewing our ass. He is more stoned than we are – gives us each a pull of his brandy.

SH2 Pytlik runs the ships store. I buy his writing paper, Christmas cards and record albums. There is perfume to send your girl. Sometimes the perfume gets as far as your rack. Scented sheets are a thrill in a roomful of beer farts. Pytlik is base barber to a company of men in a hurry to grow their hair long. He sports his own surfer bang.

One of the few advantages of ice duty is relaxed grooming rules. You can grow a beard but haircuts should be regulation. I would have to ship over to grow a beard. Traditionally the haircut rule is on hold during the winter. During my two -year career, I've avoided whitewalls except for boot camp.

11/17. On Suicide Hill, we are in the company of our hippie supply officer, Mr. Flick. He goes down the mountainside on an inner tube. Phil follows in his own tube. Mac and Kindenberg try a sled and roll it over halfway down. I go last. I wipeout into a snowdrift so deep it swallows my wallet. Mac and Kindenberg get dropped at sick bay. We are sure we will be written up for this but we want to have fun while the sun is up.

11/18. I see Mac in the galley wearing a wrist cast and a sling. Water hours are over so we are free to take showers. After work I use the head at Bldg155. Back at the firehouse, I sit atop our American La France, a white fire engine parked beneath the hot air vent that warms our garage. I feel like I'm drying my hair with a heat gun. Hooray I'm short for mess-cooking.

John is a 3rd class storekeeper, soft-spoken, non-aggressive, a stick in the snow, so to speak. He doesn't like working outdoors. He's an inside man he explains to Chief Zinmeister. He feels strongly enough about the issue to outright refuse to comply. Chief Z. has issued a direct order go out and shovel snow with the rest of his mates. There is no brig here; you don't get shot for not following orders because there are no guns and we're not at war. No Chief wants a charge that doesn't follow orders.

"Make coffee," Chief Z tells John.

"I don't drink coffee."

"I wasn't taking a fucking census. Make the coffee."

In the Navy your most important relationship is with your immediate supervisor. If you bump heads with your Chief, he has a thousand ways of bringing you into line. Transferring you to another department is the most obvious.

John gets banished from the Storekeeper hut and assigned to Bldg 155, the same building he sleeps in. He is folding bed sheets to Navy specifications. He's the designated barracks cleaner. Other men might be shamed at being made the cleaning lady but not John.

"I'm not in the same room with that prick anymore," John crows.

"You're a contentious objector," I assure him.

Back at the firehouse Les and Andy show up with two movies; The Good Bad, and the Ugly and Valley of the Dolls. We stay up till 0400.

11/20. My last day as a mess cook, from now on, when I go to 155 - a building so nondescript it is named for a number – I go as part of the general population. As a midnight treat, I have a great wet dream.

The challenge at the firehouse is to keep busy. Firemen don't have down time. They are always "in training". It works well if you are above third class. The third class keeps his strikers doing anything but sitting on their ass. The second class assists the third class by dreaming up make-work projects. Being the lowest ranked man in the house, I can't be caught doing nothing. Chores I dream up have an advantage over ones assigned me. Often I'm sent on pointless errands when I seem to be standing around. Given the opportunity, I am willing to disappear.

"Honey -bagging" is my standard response if quizzed about what I'm doing. I wire brush Ansul bottles, spray paint anything lying around and finish the last half of each shift wiping down the fire trucks. Our schedule is exact as a monastery and we are monks of fire-fighting. Butch and Les bring over a movie called "<u>In Like Flint</u>."

We often approach a standstill. If there is no productive activity on the menu my time still must be accounted for. I sign up for PACE classes in History and Philosophy, volunteer to type Homer's requisitions and lobby for a radio show. Being assigned the overnight watch keeps my work day down to four hours and a field day. It's still a challenge to stay active. Is it my fault, things don't catch fire?

11/21. Andy and I are sent out of the house to do fire inspections. That means find somewhere else to screw off. We can't think of anything to do and it's early in the summer. What happens during the winter? We sleep in John's room and then return to the firehouse for field day. There's a game of 500 Rummy going on in the kitchen.

You can't complain of being self-deprecating – no one asked you to deprecate - if you do clean it up. I'm combining philosophy, porn, Meher Baba and observations on human behavior into a three hour radio show interrupted by pretty much the same play list. I'm a sailor, a fireman and a fill in DJ. Can I get any colder?

The firehouse has a pool table and Bldg.155 has two. Why guys from 155 come over and play pool on our table is one concern Chief Wright has to deal with. He's a black Chief in a mostly white firehouse. In a parallel universe guys our age are being killed every day.

Our pool table is the compact model you find at your corner tavern. Eight ball is the standard fare. If you don't touch the eight ball when it's your only ball left, you lose. There are no written rules. Guys can Jap you by leaving their balls all over the table. I play fair, sober. When high, I think I play great. Ping pong is popular in Bldg 155 – I suck at ping pong- excuse me- tennis table - if you're a lifer.

I draw money from disbursement and go to beer sales. I can leave a case under my rack and it stays drinking cold. I use beer as a nightcap. Kees and Al get drunk after dinner. Kees is white from Texas, Al is black from Philadelphia. I join them for one Pabst before turning in. Darden can't sleep from the raised voices at the beer summit. He's out of his rack screaming for quiet. I put my head under my scented pillow.

11/25. Italian night, we skip the pasta and the movie War and Peace. Mac, Andy and I drop THC. You don't want to eat when you're buzzed. Everything is fun and funny. You have a heat rush in your chest as if you'd chugged a quart of hot soup. It keeps you awake all night which is good because you can't sleep anyway. Joe, Les and Butch are also tripping. I have a great time letting the party flow around me. I'm at sea in good company. Britain takes a hit to see what all the fuss is about. Andy and I play pool and he talks about Toms River, New Jersey where he grew up to be a petty criminal and work in an egg factory. He got married before we deployed, his girlfriend is pregnant. He'll be a father the next time he sees her. We go to bed at 0500 on Thanksgiving morning.

Mail Call 11/29... My sister Susie

Peter,

Hi-got your amusing letter today and it was good to hear from you. I'm really mad at Mom though – I had to work till 3.00pm today and when I got home I found out she had already opened your letter and read it to everyone. I'm so mad I'm still not talking to her. It's not that your letter was very personal or anything but it's the principal of the thing. Right?

Thanksgiving was pretty good but too quiet. Of course during the afternoon we watched March of the

Wooden Soldiers which makes it around the 50th time for me and then Pop and Aunt Florence came over for awhile. Tommy and Anna came for dinner – they had already eaten at her house but they sat and watched us. Must have been a lot of fun for them! I hate Tommy's hair –it's really long and it goes into a flip. Now he has a moustache too- that isn't bad but the hair has to go.

Got our report cards and of course I came shining through with an 85 average. Actually I should not have gotten that but since I'm taking typing for the second time I got a 96. I'm going to kill my English teacher though, he gave me 75 and I figured I'd be getting about 85. We only had one report and one test. I got a B+ on the report and thought I did pretty well on the test. I don't answer too much in class but that shouldn't matter too much.

It's Saturday night and as usual there's nothing to do. I should have gone to meet the kids after work but I'm too lazy to get dressed. Last night I went to a dance which was really bad. I felt like a chaperone at an eighth grade party. The band is fabulous but I could have killed these kids. I think from now on I'll just have to pass up these groovy dances.

Last Monday I went with this kid Billy to a group session thing at Molloy. It was pretty good. There were only ten kids and the Brother who was really nice. Each one of us had to say what our goals are and tell something about ourselves. The kids were all nice and I didn't feel stupid at all. Everyone else knew each other but they made me feel right at home – maybe that's why I wanted to leave right away (only kidding of course).

Mary Lou called tonight and said her Thanksgiving was pretty nice – the officers served them dinner and they were allowed to have as much as they wanted. She said she's getting everyone's letters but doesn't get a chance to write back.

I can't believe Christmas is in a couple of weeks. I don't know what to get anyone. Mom's sending your package out one of these days – I think my present will keep you busy for awhile – I think you'll find it pretty frustrating. Well I think I'd better go and get my beauty sleep (okay no wisecracks)

Love Susie

P.S. Everyone says hello and they will write soon.

11/29. Firehouse routine is precise. We break for lunch together and we wipe down the trucks every afternoon. Each of us is expected to bond with a piece of equipment. Our white American LaFrance is our leading lady. In the front seat you are looking at a cockpit full of controls and gauges. I stake out my corner on the driver's side tailgate. I'm trying to learn to drive a Nodwell, a box-like truck with tank tracks but I mess up when Conrad or Darden accompany me. When I drive truck 3 to the dump and back, without incident, I'm allowed to paint Kathy's name on the side door. She writes me every day, it's the least I can do.

Mail Call 12/1/70...Robbie Robinson

Hey Pete,

I guess today was about the best day I've had. I got your letter and one from both of my sisters and two from Joyce.

Joyce's excuse for not writing was that she was sick. I don't believe her though. So I'm not writing to her anymore.

Both of my sisters are engaged to get married.

Not much is happening around here. My day just consists of the regular mess cook chores and a movie in the evening. So you can get the picture of how much excitement there is in this camp, I spend the majority of my leisure time racked out.

I had a run in with Debellis on Thanksgiving Day. He got pissed because I told him he was doing something wrong. So he stormed out of the galley and told me to cook the fucking dinner myself. Then he came back in and told me "One of these days I'm going to bash your head in with a rolling pin, Robinson." So I told him "Let's go outside" and he declined my challenge.

I've only had one other fight. That was with Mr. Hollywood. He threw a glass of water in my face trying to act cute. So I had to warm his ass up.

Our boy Farmer has not dropped me a line in any way, shape or form. My sister hasn't sent me anything either so I've really just given up all hope

Tell Toussaint I said "Hi" and to send me them pictures. Tell him Debellis told me about him and Brenda Smith. Tell him it don't mean nothing because I've been that way myself.

Well I guess I will be seeing you in Feb, buddy. Oh yes, about them Chiefs, they did not come down here last year.

Well easy now, take care and don't let anyone get next to you.

Your number one ace - Robby

12/3. Word is passed that a BM2 McCauley is moving into the firehouse and one of us is to transfer to the crash shack at Willie Field. Andy volunteers and leaves an hour later. I think Andy and I are pretty good friends. We had one conversation that turned into a shoving match but it wasn't serious. Other than a momentary drop in temperature nothing came of it. When a guy pushes you, you push back – that's a basis of a relationship. Whatever you give me I'm giving back.

I like Andy because I think he likes me. I consider him enlightened in that respect. I have the only pot, pills and Visine in the firehouse so what's not to like about me? With Andy leaving I take over his radio show which makes me a starter as opposed to a fill in. At the firehouse Kees tells me the power went out, so I did my first scheduled show on a dead mike.

12/4. BM3 McCauley moves in and takes Andy's rack. He is the oldest sailor I have ever worked with. Story goes, he's a lifer who's been busted down a half dozen times, all alcohol related. Someone must have thought it amusing to send him to the ice where there's plenty to drink and plenty of time to drink it. He arrives with a great white beard in a town with a surplus of Hemingways. I've been here two months and I've only grown the blueprint for a red mustache.

A line from the Captain Scott's Antarctic expedition diary praising his crew, describes the McMurdo firehouse "-universally amicable spirit shown on all occasions." Allow for the occasional shoving match and that's pretty much us.

12/5. Chiefs are smarter than officers and most of them have been around longer. The officers aren't stupid; they let the chiefs run the show. I muster for Charity snack hours. We hand out beer and soda to the late shifts. Working alongside me is our Executive Officer. There is less space between officers and enlisted here than you'd find at most any other command, outside a submarine.

The firehouse has a revolving watch, six four hour shifts. As low man on the totem polar, I draw the 0300-0700 watch. While on duty I'm expected to be up and about. I'm charged with waking the Chief at 0700. I write letters, read and play solitaire on the kitchen table and then wander around town looking for fire. It's good if you can find someone to shoot the shit with but I don't mind walking alone, stranger in a strange world. I'm living aloud in the company of Mt. Erebus, Observation Hill and Hut Point. Scott and Shackleton patrolled these precincts back when exploring was still a career. When I can find good packing, I throw snowballs at telephone poles. The sun is out all through my shift so it's easy to keep an eye on town. When I do a three hour radio show before my shift, it's understood that I can sleep till lunch.

12/5. My mail makes Kees mail sick. I get letters at every mail call from my girlfriend Kathy. My Mom and Dad write me separately, my classmate from "A" school, Tom Z writes, my brother Tom writes, my sisters write if my Mom puts a gun to their heads. My friend Jim Krasowski writes letters that read like term papers. Kees gets squat. It's embarrassing to be standing next to him with a mitt full of letters. Kees is my third class. When I screw up he answers for it. I sense he has problems at home. For him, McMurdo might have advantages over Job Corps, Texas.

He tells me a story about a shipmate who dropped a letter over the side of the ship expecting Kees, who was suspended in a Bosin chair, to catch it. When the letter flutters past him and into the drink, Kees makes them lower him to the waterline to retrieve it. He's serious about mail.

We watch a movie called Kiss Kiss Kill Kill. There's a movie every night in the firehouse and on weekends a double feature. At lunch people will ask about that night's feature. It's academic; whatever it is, we're watching it. There's no TV. Depending on the projectionist you can take a dump during the change of reels. When I go back to my rack I can still hear the movie playing in the next room. I might not listen but I'll hear it.

We're on a continent with no borders containing no countries and no native population. Everybody here is a trespasser. What we carry in we are to carry out. The nuclear power plant up on the hill is our Mother. Other than our shuttle bus we are a world without public transportation.

12/5. In an effort to sleep I use Visine at bedtime. Eye drops should not be dismissed as a sleeping-aid. The liquid allows the eyelids to lower, smooth as automatic garage doors. It's the reverse of crying yourself to sleep. Before I fall off I take stock – have I been an asshole today? Who do I need to write to? Along with everyone else, I number the days.

Meher Baba has a presence in town. Two or three guys wear his lapel button. Officer Flick, a couple of radiomen and John can be caught reading his catechism. He's the guru of Pete Townsend from The Who.

"Don't worry-be happy" is Baba's motto. Borrowing a theme from Dale Carnegie's Stop Worrying and Start Living he is an Indian motivational non-speaker. I've read enough of his stuff to believe that anyone you meet in life might be God, looking for someone to believe in him. He intends to judge you on how you treat him. Psychedelics have enlightened me to the degree that I serve as my own guru and a pain in the ass to everyone else. I use mescaline and THC with the hope that mind expansion leads to a spiritual appreciation of whatever surrounds me, down to the lowest paid iceberg. Buzzed, I see everything connecting; sober I'm uncertain of things I've eye-witnessed.

12/5. Saturday afternoon, I'm in my rack doing crosswords. It's so quiet you can hear the wind outside. In my head I imagine Vietnam. The tans, the beaches, the girl-women, base camps where you can smoke pot and fire artillery. Down here I'm safe and warm in a freezing climate. I'm obliged to appreciate my circumstances despite the chill in the air and no trace of mama-san. I suspect I'd be enslaved if I were to come face to face with that conical cap witch Butch urges me to worship.

We have to touch (ha ha) on the subject of masturbation. I'm a young man locked down in an all male world. Attending to one's tempers is a personal issue. Frank and I are the only ones I know who even discuss the subject. Franks swings his legs off his rack and stands to stretch.

"No sense putting this off." He is going to lock himself in the head.

"Clean up after, okay."

"Remember the girl in the movie last night?"

"Frank is there anything you can't jerk off to?'

"Gospel music."

Our head/bathroom is on the first deck/floor at the bottom of the ladder/stairs. It's a single-hole latrine with no amenities beyond toilet paper. It's a suitable arena for two indoor sports. I cast my ballot in the same voting booth as Frank.

Pornography is scarce and the few magazines I brought here I keep hidden. You might find a Playboy lying around but anything stronger is kept undercover. Tim Hobson has a snapshot of his Japanese bar girl wife that he'll let you look at for a beer. You get busy right afterwards like an idea that demands to be jotted down.

Tom Conrad is a second class damage control man. He's more mental than mentor to me. His nickname "Arfy" was around long before I met him. After two months in the firehouse he requests a transfer to the carpenter shop because no one calls him by his real name. The Chief rips into us at muster.

"I want that nickname shit-canned starting now. I'm not going to transfer a qualified second class over this chicken shit. Do you guys want to lose your projectionist?"

Mail Call 12/8/70... My brother Tom

Dear Peter

Hello again – got your letter a few days ago & seeing as though I didn't mail the last one I wrote you, I decided to rap some more.

You letter was really interesting especially that part about the price of shit on the ice. Wow man - I have a proposition that might bring us both a nice piece of change. Dig it, in a week or so I'm probably gonna run into a lot of good shit – red hash. Right now it looks like a definite thing but you never know until it actually happens. If and when I do get it, I'm sure I can figure out a safe way of mailing some to you without the both of us getting busted.

There are a few ways possible. Hollowing out a large candle inserting some hash in it then sealing it is one of the best ways. It's supposed to be near impossible to detect the scent of hash when hidden in wax. Well anyhow, that's not really important right now and those details could always be worked out later.

If you are interested write back after you've given it some thought. If you're willing to go along- this would be the best time cause of Christmas packages. I'll wait to hear from you before I write you the details.

Wow man. I've been trying to get this letter and package off to you for a while now. I'm really stoned tonight and didn't feel at all like crashing. You asked about Michael – just the other day I got a letter from him saying all was "well". It's really strange because he's a sniper now and it blows my mind to think he might have to use all that knowledge about killing that's been drummed into his head. Me and Eddie sent him a package consisting of a gallon of Bali-hi and a whole bunch of candy. Bob Provoost wrote me about a week and a half ago and sounded pretty down regarding his court martial that was to be held a week from then. So he's already had his day in court but I haven't heard of anything since. Anna also asked me to say hello and Merry Christmas and that kinda stuff. She's sending you a card so I don't know why I just went through all this.

Tonight I received answers from Mary Lou and Artie. They both freaked me out in succession. Wow man I really don't know how to act any more. I wanted to relate to someone about how weird the whole thing was. I read Mary Lou's letter first only to find out that "Everything's fine and I really like it a whole lot."

Dig it, she explains about what she does all day and then gets into this –"I've been getting quite a lot of mail and Dad writes me all the time from his office so I can write to him there so Mom can't read them. I always could talk more to Dad than Mom."

"At any rate, Dad wrote and said in his letter that he's very worried about you and that you may be involved with the drug scene. Of course I told you weren't but he's very very worried. He practically begged me to stay away from that stuff and I told him I would (at

least while I'm here) but Tom please take care of yourself and don't get very involved in it. Besides Daddy worrying so am I. I don't want you getting in any trouble."

At this point I found myself gawking at the ceiling and remembering what you said about Mom thinking I'm a junkie. It was strange!! Thinking that must have been the highlight of Mary Lou's letter I went back to reading it. She went on –

"I was seeing a lot of a guy named Bob Sweeney before I left and I get a letter from him every day. He wants to marry me as soon as possible and get me out of here. He says he can't live without me, he misses me so much. Outrageous – I bet you never thought your ugly little sister would ever amount to anything and I would wind up as an old maid but I fooled you. I'm a WAC and really proud of it and Bob wants to marry me! (I may turn out an old maid anyway cause I'm not going to do it- marry him)."

She told me to say hello to Anna and then signed off. I sat puzzled about the whole thing for a long time. It was a while before I picked up Artie's letter and tore into it. He explained what he does all day and that he's been training with mortars for a couple of weeks. "It looks 100% definite that I'll be going to Vietnam – it may not be bad if I stay a mortar man."

I started to realize the similarities between the two letters. It really started to get freaky when he wrote – "I know what you mean about how strange things seem compared with a few years ago. I remember how things were, say like before I went away to college and its unbelievable how much things have changed since then. I would never have believed that a few years later Peter would be in Antarctica and Mary Lou in the WACs. (I'm still not too sure I believe that one yet). It's been a hassle just being away all the time for the last six years and I'm not looking forward to being away for a couple more. Regina and I would like to get married sometime but the Army sort of interferes with that."

Before he signed off he asked "How's Anna doing —tell her I said hello. I wondered what the hell was happening and I still am. I don't know if I'm exaggerating the importance of these raps cause I'm stoned, real stoned and they're flipping me out. I compared the letters again and noticed a few more coincidences. In her letter Mary Lou says "I'll be home Dec. 17 to Jan 3rd." Artie writes "I've gotten tickets home already for Christmas. I'll be home on Dec. 17th. I'll be glad when I get out of here."

Wow man, this must all sound pretty strange to you but like I said before I wanted to relate this to someone and I think you're the only person that would understand. I really don't understand myself so I'm gonna change the subject. Besides it's getting too far out and I'm having trouble putting down what I'm thinking.

It's getting pretty late and I have to get up tomorrow morning so I'm gonna try to crash. If you don't understand what this letter is all about don't worry cause I don't think I do myself. Well I just can't concentrate on it anymore so be good and stay out of trouble.

Tom

P.S. Don't forget about writing back your answer. Say hello to everybody. - Peace.

In that same mail call I get a letter from McNally who's camped on a rainy hillside in the central highlands. He mentions causalities being carried on ponchos. Down here we're concerned with an outbreak of nicknames. I've gotten other letters from Jim Lettis and Dennis Nagle – guys I grew up with who are now in the war thanks to the draft. I congratulate myself on joining the Navy but still feel like I'm missing a party. Krasowski writes from Germany. Kees gets a Christmas card from the Sweeney, Texas VFW.

12/9. I seem to be a hamster running on a wheel. I go from the firehouse to the chow hall to the radio station and nowhere else. I'm feeling a touch of wanderlust when Conrad asks me to go with him to retrieve a fire sled left at an equipment yard outside of town. He doesn't order me to go but I'm restless enough to agree. Dad advised me not to volunteer for anything until I was certain it would be assigned to me -sort of why I joined the Navy.

We drive the Nodwell, a tank without a turret and gun. You use two upright levers to steer. Conrad drives while I try to spot the sled. We have the heater blasting and my window open. I stare at the ice shelf - an expanse of white stage suitable for a dinosaur musical. I imagine Brontosauruses on their hind legs twirling in tutus. We get lost and wind up driving all the way to the Kiwi base where our arrival calls for a good laugh and a shot of brandy. On the way back to base, Conrad lets me drive. In the rear view mirror I see the metal ribs that secure our tracks flying off into the snow. We're stuck in a real middle of nowhere in a tank with a flat. I regret my restlessness.

We radio the firehouse and the Chief drives out to rescue us. Sitting in the truck with the heat on puts us both to sleep. We get driven back to the firehouse, issued replacement parts and brought back. No help from our mates. Its 1800 and the sun stands guard in the middle of the sky. We're expected to repair the truck and get it back to base. I've never done this kind of work, replacing the metal slats that splice the track together. One of us has to sit on the ground and align the holes in the track using a marlin spike. The guy up top sinks a bolt that pushes the spike out. From the bottom, a ratchet wrench nuts the bolt. The two levels of track and the rib flatten as a Cuban sandwich. Three bolts per rib and 12 ribs to install, we are swearing, cursing and dropping parts in the snow.

Chief Wright is testing Conrad's leadership skills and I'm playing the part of a lab rat. I'll work just as hard as the next guy. If given the chance to skate, I'll take it.

There's been many times when I've busted my ass while watching other guys slide. If you're freezing your ass off you tend to work quick. If it was up to me we would leave the Nodwell out on the ice until every possible resource could be brought into the effort to rescue her. My mates don't agree. No one comes out to assist us.

Progress is slow and we have to get back in the truck and warm up every fifteen minutes. As junior man I get the sit-on-snow responsibility. It takes three hours to get the first four ribs in place. Rather than defer to Conrad who seems unsure of what we're doing, I start to take charge. While Conrad is on the ground I wrestle with the track on top. Over the sound of the running motor I hear him snoring. He's fallen asleep under the Nodwell. I start screaming at him.

"No one is coming to help us. We've gotta get out of this place."

When finished we limp back to the firehouse at 0600. Twelve hours of dicking around in the great outdoors has me intoxicated. In the firehouse kitchen, I add a line to the daily log. WE FINALLY FUCKING MADE IT!

12/9. Mr. Pruitt, our department officer, conducts an ass chewing about the integrity of a Navy log. It's directed at me but since Darden was holding the watch, the log is his responsibility. Darden glares at me as I try to explain away a very bad mood. Nothing comes of it except shit details for a guy who does shit details. What else can they do - bust me down to E-1? You're not allowed outdoors if you're not at least an E-2.

We get to phone patch home via a ham radio network. If atmospheric conditions allow we can talk to our girl friends and families back in the states. You talk as a telegram ending each remark by saying "Over". This signals the party you have called that it's their turn to talk.

Kees gets a phone number via Hobson's wife and calls his girlfriend Susie at the Happy Bar in Sasebo, Japan. He tells us she doesn't speak much English and only asks "Billy when you come?" We get a big kick out of repeating that line when we're not quoting <u>Cool Hand Luke.</u>

Kees's sense of humor goes pretty far. You can kid him but don't trash his ship the Navasota. Andy suggests that the Vietnam War will be over before the "Never Sober" arrives. "That ship got passed by Kon-Tiki."

 Kees stabs our kitchen table with a hunting knife during a debate about firehouse responsibilities. He shows me a hammer he carries around because a Second Class is riding his ass. Being a Texan, we aren't sure what he's capable of. He tells me a story of being assigned to stand watch at a deserted barracks at boot camp. They forgot he was there and marked him AWOL. Thirty six hours later they find him holding post. A madman when mad he's a good ole boy otherwise. He played defensive line on the undefeated high school football team - the Sweeney Bulldogs. 450 points on offense – defense gave up 36 - during a16-0 championship season. He is 5'10 on tiptoe and a big fat lie at 185lbs but he took every snap as a starter.

12/10. Al Saunders puts a sign in the firehouse kitchen - Anyone Who Leaves the Sink Dirty – Spends the Night in the Box –another nod to Cool Hand Luke. I have a regular radio show now. Between songs I try comedy. "A Polish guy is asked to read an eye chart. He says "Hey I know this guy."

Kees is my closest mate and my third class. He tries to keep me out of trouble. He told me not to write that line in the log book – at twenty one I have listening issues. He doesn't approve of guys getting high but he isn't going to bust those of us who do. When a "base wide" drug raid is announced the firehouse is the only place that gets searched. I have been given enough notice to move my stash to the Storekeepers hut. Kees and I got high in Davisville so he doesn't want to bust me or the girls in my sewing circle. When drunk, Homer insists Kees restrain us.

"Take my crow Homer- I'm not playing hall monitor."

12/11. It's snowing like crazy and Christmas is coming to a town full of Santas. The sun is awake behind a shower curtain. There's a shuttle bus between McMurdo and Willie Field that carries mail and breakouts. We plan a road trip to the strip to visit with Andy. We hear it's a snow white Wild West town with a free for all sleep cycle and limited lifers. Nobody is enforcing the haircut policy out there. Other than here, it's the only other place we can be.

Cynthia Meyers's flesh has the hue of new lumber. Her Playboy centerfold (December 1968) has been my girl on paper from Newport to Davisville to McMurdo. When I'm pretty sure I won't be uprooted, I hang her on the wall above my rack. Guys mock her 39DD breasts. Posed on her knees, the camera looking down, her twins appear as blonde seal pups breaking through the icecap of her ribcage.

"Why not pin up a picture of Elsie the cow?"

"Can she even see her feet?"

I endure insults on her behalf. The fewer men who pay her tribute allow me more opportunities to offer praise. She's all girl and her big brown eyes possess me as much as her dangling chandeliers. Those airbags have seduced the most famous tit men of my era; Hugh Hefner and the film director, Russ Meyer – no relation.

Around her tri-fold I create a montage of what I find erotic. There's not much stimuli lying around McMurdo. I have my girlfriend's photo, a couple of magazines and a pocket sized sex novel. I hang the Vargas girls from Playboy as wallpaper. Along with my roommates, I string bird cloth across my rack for privacy.

12/13. When we reach the crash shack we interrupt a game of Acey Deucey. After an hour I'm up $16 and we break to get high. Jack, Andy and Teddy take half-tabs of mescaline. John and I each do a hit of THC. A few joints appear and the party is on. We're laughing and carrying on over nothing funny but everything hysterical. There's a half ass attempt to play a card game called Bullshit. It requires pulling each other back into the present moment at every deal. I'm so zonked that I can only stare at my chow. At 2030 we're back on the shuttle bus to McMurdo. We arrive to mail and Christmas packages –today is a day that stands out in a string of days that don't.

If you've never met a little guy who tries to bully a giant let me introduce my penis. Regardless of schedule this brat insists on a five minute solo at least once a day. Frank and I are the only two guys I know who commiserate on the demands of masturbation. Why is it a taboo subject? Guys get insulted if you call them jerk-offs or wankers.

My brother was on a high school religious retreat when he opened a Bible that was inscribed "I was a slave to masturbation when I got here, now I am the master of it."

I don't hear guy says "Suck my dick," like they do in the regular navy. It's not done here. In the real world you're obligated to connect with the opposite sex so it's unacceptable to jerk off in Davisville. At McMurdo, we're up and about under an insomnia sun that makes getting to sleep an uphill issue. Any activity that helps you relax should be considered therapeutic. I believe a man should shave his temper to make himself a more acceptable neighbor in a small world. If you can't summon a wet dream take matters in your own hand. It makes you easier to live with.

Officer Elkins tells me, straight-faced, that my not having a regulation haircut detracts from our mission in Antarctica.

"We're here to raise standards not relax them," I'm told. I may do the same work but the guy with the whitewalls is the real Navy. Long hair is an irritant to most lifers; others just love to enforce rules. Non-regulation hair indicates rebellion, drug use and an anti-war mentality.

Schools like Sweeney High were in the forefront of LBJ's integration program. When the local black high school merged with the white high school, Kees found out he was understudy to a black defensive tackle.

"Heard you're second string to a nigger," his Dad asked.

"Who told you that?"

"You're not living here if you are."

Kees came to the next practice tackling anything that moved. His coach couldn't get him off the field. He wouldn't go home until the he was listed as a starter. His Dad nodded approval.

I should emphasize that there is no smoking in bed at McMurdo. Any drunk NCO falls asleep and sets his mattress on fire becomes the business of the McMurdo Fire Department. Guys lose a stripe for a bad night. Every man is expected to control his temperature in and out of bed.

"Are you going for a swim?" I ask Frank.

"I went earlier with your book

My paperback copy of The Debauched Hospodar by Guillaume Apollinaire is the cornerstone of my erotica cache. It's connoisseur quality, underground, over-the-top, turn of the century, porn in print. Guillaume's appetites are revealed through the exploits of his handsome hero, the Prince Mony Visbcu.

Hospodar is an administrative title equivalent to County Executive. His father held the title but Mony upgraded to the simpler, Prince. At every turn of page his indulgences assault the reader.

Apollinaire was a French poet who moved among the Paris avant-garde during its fling with the "new spirit" movement. He couldn't paint so with words he tried to shock as a Picasso of prose. He championed the school of "Cubism" and applauded the scorn of popular convention in art. I know because I read it in the Grove Press forward. I have to really like a book to read the forward.

12/15/70 Mail Call... My Dad.

Dear Peter,

I have the letter you mailed November 25th responding to my spate of letters. I found it interesting in that I believe that, although we still seem to be circling around throwing feints, we are coming closer to a worthwhile exchange of ideas. It has been said many times that the Bible can be used to prove any point but I think you are off base when you refer to the parable of the Good Shepherd. The point of the parable is made by Christ when he says the repentance of one sinner is greater than all those in no need of repentance. In connection with the situation concerning Tom, I prefer the parable of the prodigal son whose father receives him with open arms after he has sown his wild oats. The door here is always open to Tom and he could even move back in if he chose but it would mean his conforming to the lifestyle of this home.

That you should be shocked at our reasons for asking him to conform or live elsewhere surprises me. My concern for the younger children, especially John, left me no choice. To get Biblical again (you started it) "He that should scandalize one of the little ones...it would be better for him that a millstone should be hanged around his neck etc etc." You understand that John is my son. I'm responsible for his upbringing and I can't have my philosophy undermined by a surrogate father whose views on life seem so far at variance to my own. In addition it was an absolute choice based on the pragmatic approach of the greater good for the greater number. Your Mother's mental and physical health was being affected and if anything happened to her this family would disintegrate. It may seem callous but life has seemed much more serene with four older children out on their own. If anyone is rolling in at 5AM, getting drunk or high on drugs, wrecking cars etc. we are not spending sleepless nights worrying ourselves to death. Maybe it's a case of what you don't know doesn't hurt you.

 I can't really respond as you would like me to concerning the drug scene. I resent of course being accused of getting my ideas from magazines but you are not the first one to make that pitch. Many people can't give anyone credit for original ideas. Sure everyone tends to read periodicals that bolster one's beliefs and I only point out that your recommending Leary and Playboy fall into the same pattern. I am sure if the Playboy article condemned all drug use you wouldn't recommend it. It never ceases to amaze me when I hear young people who couldn't manage a C in high school chemistry speaking authoritatively on the various effects of hallucinogens – all parroted from the latest publication of some instant authority.

It's bad enough to have Tom defend marijuana as not harmful (he may have a point but it is far from proven) but to have you suggest that drugs are a positive *good is hard to swallow. All medicines are dangerous in inexperienced hands even though they may be life-savers when used properly. You ask an awful lot if you want me to go along with the idea that anyone is capable of deciding how and when to use LSD, mescaline or speed. The public lives of both Leary and Pike are hardly likely to command anyone's confidence - unless someone is looking for some authority to support a preconceived notion.*

I have always had too much respect for my mind and body to really appreciate people who tamper with theirs. Take alcohol –you know I drink but I have rarely gotten drunk and never when it would have affected my competence. During the war, I was detailed to take out a platoon to blow up a bridge (no-demine a bridge that the Germans were going to blow up.) and everyone else but me was stewed. It was one of the most frightening experiences I've had. There was no one on whom I could rely and it was my life at stake. The other guys thought it was a big picnic. Thank God the Jerries blew the bridge before we got there. I have never forgotten that night – I learned how dangerous things that becloud your mind or senses can be. Just imagine a fire on the ice where lives depended on you and your mates. What would happen if you were all on a trip – when you were needed?

I don't buy your implied criticism that I decided Tom was on narcotics without proof. We are not dealing with a court case and innocent until proven guilty stuff. I <u>knew</u> it without having absolute proof just as I know you have experimented with drugs and so has Mary Lou (at least marijuana). You ask why I didn't help him. No one can be helped unless they want to be helped. He didn't want to be helped because he figured he didn't need help. Like you he thought drug use beneficial or at least harmless.

Remember Tom was 22 when he left home – he was no kid. He was a man and had to be treated like a man. He was welcome to stay in this house provided he understood it was our house (your Mother's and mine) and that our rules governed the way life was lived. The decision to leave had to be his even though it was on an "or else" basis. He was a man with a decision to make between two options. He made it.

The point you make about music, art and cinema being hobbies is great if you follow through with the reasoning. They should be hobbies; that's all. When they become the end-all of life something is out of joint. To ascribe some mystical religious meaning to rock music is making the same mistake that guys did twenty or thirty years ago about jazz music.

I do have a tendency to reject anything that is anti-social. I don't say anti-establishment because 'establishment' is a sort of code word which nobody ever defines. It's a handy non-word that can be used to replace logical thought because it means whatever the listener wants –like "relevant" "now" "right on" and a host of others. I reject anti-social attitudes because I'm part of society and anything anti-social is anti-me. If society is destroyed I go down with it.

Slipping the blade about the early Christians doesn't become you. Dialogue on religion must presume a common belief. The early Christians were not anti-establishment in the sense you use it. They had a vision of an after-life (how many hippies do today?) and cared nothing for trying to make a Utopia on earth. They refused to worship Ceasar because of a belief in God. That made them lawbreakers the same as being a priest in England during Elizabeth's reign made a man an outlaw. There are few revolutionaries today who are out for the honor and glory of God.

You have always felt that you must do what you believe in. "This above all, to thy own self be true." Give me the same understanding. When it came to a head about Tom playing my game or finding his own place I did the only thing I could and still retain my own self-respect, despite the heartache it caused me. It is easy to talk about what you should do in any given situation but it's not so easy when it comes time to put your money where your mouth is.

Well I have to stop sometime so III cut it short here. I enjoy these conversations very much and I hope you do. I know I must seem intransigent but despite what impression you may have, I have spent a good deal of my life thinking about serious things and I do not find my beliefs easily shaken.

Love Dad

12/16. Frank is a country boy, Erwin, Tennessee, blonde with a bony build. His seat pants suggest an empty mailbag. His girlfriend's picture is in a frame beside his rack. When I can find a photo of a black guy in a magazine, I cut it out and tape it to her picture. Frank has a great sense of humor unless you trash LSU. He once phoned-patched his Dad and complained of being pale.

"Now don't you worry about that none, Son."

Frank mutters while stirring grits on the firehouse stove. He fights his own farts with a can of air freshener. He's a third class Boatswain Mate; the Navy's most hard ass rating.

There's a basketball hoop above the door inside the firehouse. With the trucks outside we play half-court. Chief Wright and I challenge Saunders and Kees. If you want competitive basketball split up the black guys. Kees is a good athlete. I'm enthusiastic, no one keeps score.

12/17. Al Saunders checks out. The firehouse will be quieter without him. The other day Butch was busting Al's balls by claiming he was the only black guy he knew who ate pussy. Al threw a temper tantrum over it. Chief Wright came into our room to say, "I didn't know there was anything wrong with it."

He turns to me for support. I shrug my shoulders. I have only hearsay on the subject. Butch and Al leave the ice together. They can discourse on the subject during the eight hour flight back to the world. I give Butch $80 so he can send me drugs by mail when he gets home. Like Vietnam, guys are here one day and not the next.

Zoomie's real name is Lee. He's a skinny kid charged with finishing the summer tour of a drop-out. He lands in the firehouse two weeks before Christmas. The runt of a litter, he is passed down to the bottom of the world. When another command sends you a man, you know he's a screw up. Zoomie came here from Norfolk where he swept a Chief off his feet with an out of control floor buffer. The Chief broke his hip. The only sane reason for having him at McMurdo is to keep him away from the rest of the world. I bond with him – as long as he's here I won't be the biggest fuckup in the house. Zoomie's tour is one we count down along with him.

12/19/70 Mail Call ... Tom Z.

Pete,

I should have mailed my lifer Christmas card earlier but all last week I had to clean oil tanks. Really great for working 12 hrs a day and getting oil all over yourself. I'll ship over if I can stay on this oiler and clean tanks all year round. If they don't let me stay on this beautiful ship, I'll be getting out in 484days. This is without a cut and I better get a nice long one. Have a Merry Christmas and a Happy New Year, at least it will be a white one.

Tom

Z's greeting is on the official Christmas card of the USS Caliente. Oilers are named after rivers. Tom's name is Zmylinski - Z after the first time you meet him.

12/21. At morning quarters, we meet Al Saunders replacement; a kid just in from San Diego. His name is Jim Edwards. In Nam he would be shunned as the

FNG, at McMurdo he just settles in. If having him here makes anyone of us a day shorter- welcome aboard. He'll be staying for the overnight. I'm out of the house most of the day with Old Boats doing a zone inspection - walking around base looking for stuff to shoplift. At field day I'm sweeping the truck bay and the new guy approaches me.

"What your name?" That's exactly how he says it. Hilarious - we call him Fast Eddie. You're not on board till you get a nickname.

Frank caught a touchdown pass in a high school championship that got him red-shirted at LSU. The school invited him and his parents to a basketball home game. At halftime the public address announcer asked the crowd to give a big hand to him and his family. "We want Frank to come play for the Tigers." The crowd roared. There was never any idea of going anywhere else.

While playing high school basketball against an all black school, Frank sank a jump shot and then waved a rebel flag hankie. The crowd went ugly and Frank had to be escorted out of the gym. Frank is a sweet, funny racist- his Dad taught him.

He played the bench in basketball most of his freshman year. Despite round the clock tutoring from his girlfriend he flunked out of LSU on academics. I try to imagine how bad your grades would have to be to negate an athletic scholarship. His first assignment in the Navy was Guam. He stopped complaining about it when he got to McMurdo.

12/24 – There's a Christmas spirit among men who don't want to think about not being home for Christmas. An Admiral flies down and addresses the crew assembled on the corner of Main and Broadway. After chow John, Kees and I each do a hit of THC. This is the first time I see Kees get high on the ice. We have a great time walking around busting into people's rooms to wish them a Merry Christmas. Most everyone is drunk by 2000. I open my gifts from home. I had asked for earphones so my record player wouldn't disturb my mates. My Mother sent me earmuffs. Everyone seems to be in a great mood- it takes all night to get to sleep.

I'm reading a book, "I Don't Agree." By Noah Deal and my radio show jokes are staler than that. I pretend that the Old Man is listening because he might be - I'm on for three hours - 2400-0300.

"Got on the air late, I was teaching a Seabee to tie his shoe - Firehouse Pete on WASA your only radio station!"

The Debauched Hospodar is a slender paperback; a perfect fit for under a scented pillow. My copy includes black and white photos of naked women with 1950's school bus bushes. The text itself is a furious recount of sexual excess, not to be consumed in one sitting. Set in Bucharest during the wars that preceded World War I, the young nobleman hero sets out to conquer whatever womanhood comes his way. The boundaries of acceptable porn were yet to be defined. Apollinaire imposed no restraints on his imagination.

He describes Prince Vibescu throwing a whore back on a bed "allowing her mules to clack to the floor."

His arrangement of letters in words and words in sentences may result in the reader rubbing the text on his leg or dropping it like a hot rock. Apollinaire insists his reader either spike the book or announce himself just as depraved as the Prince.

A Paris art tart, Guy crows over his love of buggery throughout his tale. Prince Mony Vibescu makes no distinction between sexuality and homosexuality. All pleasure is justified; tastes include whipping, torture, and toilet play.

McMurdo is more snow blown than snowbound. Wind carries volcanic buckshot through town at eye level. I have to pitch forward and hold my hood down. Snowdrifts collect in the corners of buildings and along the hollows below the shoulder of the roads. The guts of our heat and light systems are above ground and protected by wooden framing. Telephone poles tilt like drink sticks. Wires bow as clotheslines down Main Street. Short staircases are built into the slopes of town. They keep you from falling on your ass when walking downhill. Base design seems random. Other than putting the dump downwind, you might describe the layout as unconsidered. An arrangement of shelters spilled from a dice cup.

There's a running dialogue about the temperature. Guys from the upper Midwest claim it was colder at home. No one cares how cold you were –we care how cold we are. It's boring to review the numbers. It's either cold or very cold and sometimes very fucking cold.

Smoking in bed and the dump fire are two concerns of the McMurdo Fire Department. Another is the nuclear power plant sitting uphill from town. The possibility of our sleep-over being micro-waved by a radiation spill is discussed in muted tones. We conduct fire drills at the plant that involve a costume change to Haz-Mat gear. As space-walkers we single file through the plant in a dress rehearsal for a real disaster.

When we have our first alarm at the nuclear plant, we charge uphill in full force. Our white American La France leads our armada followed by three Nodells, racing like box turtles alongside the Chief's jeep.

It's a false alarm but we don't know that. The thrill of hanging off the back of a fire truck under full steam with lights and sirens blasting can't be replicated - I don't care what kind of pill you're taking. Clinging to my corner of the truck like a sanitation cowboy I let one leg hang free as if skiing on air. My hat blows off.

"Kearney, where's your cover?"

"Blew off, Chief."

"Return to the house and get another."

It's a long walk back to the firehouse but it's all downhill. I pass the CO in his Jeep coming up. Our Chief will brief the Old Man. He's doesn't want to have to explain why one of his crew is out of uniform. My shock of hair is unrestrained so I take no offense. We're allowed to grow beards but summer haircuts should be regulation. I spend my days ducking officers and NCO's hot to enforce this rule.

I'm reading The Electric Kool-Aid Acid Test and listening to Pink Floyd so any sailor concerned with my interests doesn't have much of a knot to untie. The art gallery on my wall is a collage of counter culture and erotica. Lifers get a kick of sticking their heads in our sleeping quarters before the movie and wondering aloud what's become of their Navy. It's the last reel of 1970 - we're engaged in a war we can't win or get out of.

As the year rolls over, over in Nam, America's military focus switches from Cambodia to Laos. Restricted by congressional restraints we send the ARVN into Laos with a pat on the back and unlimited air support. Designated bottlenecks in the Ho Chi Minh trail are bombed every twenty minutes but not a single

American infantryman is authorized to cross the border.

In the course of clearing a path for the ARVN to enter Laos, American losses mount. Most are helicopters and Air Force fighter bombers snuffed out by ground to air missiles. War news comes to us via USO newsletters that collect at the radio station. Body counts break up love songs.

Marvin the ARVN is outfitted to the teeth with America's best equipment. The missing ingredient in his arsenal is the sense of purpose his enemy possesses. He is led by corrupt overpaid Catholic officers happy to have enlisted Buddhist troops to order into battle. Wiping out the NVA seems whimsical as eliminating rats from a Bronx housing project.

Paul Laine plays country music on his tape recorder. I'm listening to Merle Haggard and Johnny Cash, for the first time in my life. Paul is a third class who I suspect thinks of me as a pain in the ass. I have nothing against the guy but I don't defer to him because he has a higher rank. In the military that's a social blunder. Paul has good mechanical skills but little to say in the course of everyday conversation. If he does say something heads turn and stay turned until his remarks are dismissed as pointless. Paul likes to spend time playing cards or lying on his bed writing letters. He doesn't drink or do drugs as far as I know. We don't work together very often. If I want to prank someone I pick on Frank, Kees or Fast Eddie.

Homer Hall is our first class and he's going to run the show once Chief Wright is called home. As an E2 I'm aware that I should always be in motion. One duty of the Chief and Homer is to see that I advance in rank. They could assign me to hit the books for one of the Navy-wide advancement exams. I'm content with my present rank.

I joined the Navy to get laid in foreign countries. I'm getting married when my enlistment ends. Stepping on a rake – I get assigned to McMurdo. That leaves me two more years and a short time to make up for lost time. I'm not getting laid and I'm not getting shelled. We are a firehouse of spaded cats.

12/31. It's New Year's Eve and the sun is shining. Buzzed on a half-tab and a couple of beers I stand on Main Street pissing a rainbow. I raise my middle finger and hold the pose as if the subject of a photo.

1/1. The drugs I asked Butch to send arrive today. An accompanying unsigned letter describes MDA as a blend of cocaine and mescaline in pill form. The tiny purple dots are no bigger than a chip off an aspirin. There are twenty of them and a little grass included as a formality.

Psychedelics are a threat to our armed forces. You can't fight the war on LSD. The mysticism of mind expansion grinds gears with military service. You're seeing yourself on stage in a costume drama.

The parcel from Butch means 1971 will be a mind blowing year. Between shifting work schedules, radio shows, red eye, pill adventures and double features, I'm apt to be awake at any hour. After my overnight shift, I'm charged with trying to sleep through the noise of the day. While on my WASA late night radio show, I spin folk rock to sleeping Seabees. Other DJ's come up with on air names. Rich Wilson calls himself The Hawk.

"This is the Hawk talking."

1/3. John and I each take one hit of the MDA. It's Sunday and we have free time. After an initial buzz that is quite pleasant, I'm overcome with a fear of being too high. I walk to Hut Point with Kees and Mac but turn around as soon as we get there. I'm concerned with how John is doing. I find him at the GSK warehouse sitting in the dark with cat eyes flashing and his mouth open. I suggest we go outside because this ride is escalating. As soon as we are outdoors, I puke from a nervous stomach.

The effects of psychedelics vary and can be oversold. Once in awhile a sun storm will explode inside your brain that knocks your self-image into the seats around ringside. A disassembly of who you are, where you are and what you're doing commences without invitation. You sweat inside a meat bathrobe while trying to recall why you came into the world.

I feel adrenalin overcoming me and it's not pleasant. A madman has me in a rear naked choke. I'm being mugged by an evil shadow. Has Butch sent me poison? Paranoia pinches the back of my neck.

John and I start walking up Observation Hill with Mt. Erebus rumbling in our brains. We talk and walk for hours. The sun is brilliant and the landscape colorless. The primary subject we discuss is that we're never taking a hit of this shit ever again. I'm aware that the drug is in charge but I want out. There are moments when we're uncertain if we'll ever come down. After a rush comes a lull and then a bigger rush that hints of bigger rushes to come. I touch my face, convinced it's been transformed. We take turns counseling each other that there's no sense in sharing our predicament with anyone else. Sick bay won't have an antidote. We're certain the look on our faces will alarm anyone we meet.

John and I are striding uphill to escape capture. I turn to John; his face is a wind chime of mirror chips. I stare straight ahead after that. Our bond is of two people sharing a car on a rollercoaster. I'm seeing the world through a stain glass window. Door sized panels of St. Patrick green fan out in front of me like cards in a magic deck.

"Is the devil waiting for us at the top of this hill?" I ask John.

We decide we will not turn around until we have at least one foot on volcanic ground. We are stranded at sea on a leaky lifeboat where we have to depend on each other to retain our sanity. After a long afternoon our nerves are a little bit stilled. We are nowhere near the summit of the mountain we're climbing. It's moving away from us as we move toward it. Neither of us is wearing a watch and any sense of time is tits up. We're worried that we might be attracting attention by being so far away from everyone else. We hope to come down while descending.

Of all the psychedelics I have screwed around with, this one makes me turn in my Moody Blues. I swear if I ever get sober I'll stay that way. We get back to town after evening chow with no interest in eating. After hours of hanging from a windowsill by my fingertips, I swear to stay square if I ever get indoors. I'm aware of forces outside my sober self. I've peeked a curtain and felt the wind-chill.

I stay up all night in Jack's room trying to settle myself. Why take a pill when you're unsure of its effect? Is what you call adventure really self-destruction? Why scramble your own brain? I'm hearing my Dad's voice.

1/4. I'm at Chapel begging forgiveness for my reckless disregard of the gifts God has given me. I pray my balance be restored. Opening to

Deuteronomy I read "A prophet who speaks of another God will die."

By reading Meher Baba's pamphlets I have leveled nine of the Ten Commandments. As yet, I have not coveted my neighbor's ass but it's early. Winter over hasn't even started. As far as adultery goes, I've sinned a thousand times a day inside my mind. I imagine explaining to Jesus why I would give Meher Baba the time of day. He's just another guy saying he's God. Baba Ram My Ass, the Beatle's Yogi, the other fat toddler and Sai Baba - guru of baby talk - all of these Eastern life-coaches didn't help me one bit when I was sitting on that hot stove of poison pill.

1/5. I'm a zombie sailor. Kees suspects something. He's on my ass all day. Andy asks if I would send my record player out to the strip on the shuttle bus. I'm not so hung over that I agree to that. By 1600 I'm in bed and out till 0400. I consider mailing the shit back to Butch. I can't imagine why he didn't warn me to only take a half a hit. He probably never took the stuff himself- he was always a coat holder. I wouldn't say I'm fully sober yet. I can't stay mad at Kees. We walk to Hut Point to check on the progress of our visiting ships. They are baby-stepping across the Ross Sea led by Coast Guard icebreakers.

James Clark Ross was first to surf this sea. An explorer, a navigator and the man who named a mile high wall of white – The Perpendicular Barrier of Ice. The Geographic Society renamed the formation The Ross Ice Shelf.

1/6/71 Mail Call ... My brother Tom

Dear Peter

Hey Man, what goes on? I got your letter yesterday – it was really together I'm glad you dug the album – I'll send some more if you tell me what you need or what you've got. The new George Harrison is really out-a-sight, so is Jefferson Airplane's "Blows Against the Empire."

About the hash – dig it. I'm gonna mail it to you in a first class Photographs-Handle With Care" envelope. Ist Class mail isn't subject to inspection and I don't think they X-ray them because it fucks up the photographs. I don't know the exact amount yet cause I've smoked some and sold a little. When I send it I'll write the number of grams on the inside of the envelope. It'll be wrapped in cellophane so I don't think they'll detect any scent. I'll put a phony return address on the package and it'll be addressed to" P. Karney. This will clear you as far as getting busted while it's being mailed. The P could stand for Paul or Phil or Pasqualle for all you give a shit and the last named spelled wrong will legally clear you. I won't include your service number either.

As soon as you receive it, mail word to me as quickly as possible –ok. If you don't get it by Feb 1 it will probably never get there but that's the chance I'll take. I'm gonna mail it Thursday Jan 7ᵗʰ so it should arrive to you within 10 days after that. The whole purpose of this letter is to warn you in advance that it's on its way.

Thanks again for your letter. Remember to write as soon as it comes. Be good and keep the peace

Tom

P.S. Say hello to all your people and when you get the goodies have a poke on me. Bro.

1/10. I paint the white wall behind my rack black and then pull off strips of masking tape that leave a geometric design. Between the rock music and the crash pad décor I announce my space a stoner hangout. I have no idea what other people think. I expect to go on decorating until someone tells me to stop.

1/12. The Coast Guard icebreaker Burton Island calls McMurdo. Its crew abandons ship and draws a few days of shore duty. They appear crazier than us. We've been stuck in a town; they've been stuck on an icebreaker. Chief Wright takes a weekend liberty in

ChiChi - Homer is gone home on emergency leave. Our Second Class Jack runs the firehouse and we skate like the Ice-Capades. Jack doesn't care; he's not staying for the winter.

1/13. A firehouse work crew paints our pool room a combination of international orange, powder blue and black. The result is jarring enough to make you scratch the eight ball. Conrad builds a backboard for our dart board. We're gearing up for the winter. Every day the summer population ebbs away. Like Vietnam there are guys you see today you won't see tomorrow. At the outlying stations you are taking a bath in a coffee cup but here at McMurdo, I can avoid a person if I want to. That means anyone eager to get on my ass about getting a haircut. Tonight's movie features Inger Stevens in a flick called <u>Borgia Stick.</u>

1/15/71 Mail Call...My sister Susie (on personalized letterhead)

Peter,

Hi –how do you like the official paper? There was just so much fan mail for me that Mom & Dad had to do something. This way, I just autograph a couple of pieces and send them out each month – of course they aren't satisfied but they can't have everything.

Things here are going pretty well. Yesterday I heard on the radio that a plane that was flying from McMurdo to Ross Island was lost. I told Mom, so she sat in the living room and listened to the radio all day to hear about it. It didn't come on again till last night – she was going to strangle me for telling her. She acts as though I made her listen all day. Anyway it was about a helicopter that was found later on. She found an article about it in the paper and is sending it to you I think.

Mary Lou and Artie are gone. Mary Lou has not changed a bit –I don't know whether that's good or not. Artie called last night and we got the good news about Vietnam. Mom & Dad feel pretty bad (so do I, of course) but there isn't too much they can do. I still can't imagine him going. I'll be hoping to the last minute that something comes up, like NCO school or even better that the stupid war is over – nothing like hoping for everything.

New Year's Eve was pretty good. Kevin asked me out (shock of the year) for dinner and then we went to a party. I had to work that night but we closed early. He picked me up at 8.30 and we went with three other couples to this Italian restaurant, Teddy's. I had spaghetti which I couldn't even finish half of. After that we went to Richie's (his friend) house for the party. That was alright, there was a lot to drink and I think I overdid it.

Don't tell Mom.

Love

Susie.

The theme song to my radio show is The Worst That Could Happen by the Brooklyn Bridge. I'm a New

Yorker with a Yankee accent so not everyone understands me. Do I have listeners? It depends on who you ask. I try to read news items with a sarcastic tone and slip in ones I've written. Every show includes one play of James Brown's - If I Ruled the World- the only departure from my folk rock format. I still don't have an on air name- Firehouse Pete has been mocked by everyone.

Everyone knows how wrong the war is and what a waste of time, lives and money it will involve for us to save face. We need to quit without seeming to lose. The United States does not surrender. We will have to fight to finish a war we lost before it began. We're suffering for mistakes our grandfathers made. We got played by the French. How come every time there's a big war these people are in it? The best we could have done was to create a new Korea. If you're willing to accept half a baby you don't deserve a baby.

Whale sharks mate in these waters. Coasties talk of orca orgies in the newly open sound. We're seeing for the first time the cold water of the Ross Sea. Andy tells us he laid on the edge of ice shelf and looked down to see killer whales. I'm not challenging him, I love bullshit.

I sell some of the drugs Butch sent to a visiting Coastie and a couple of my town mates. I'm happy to be rid of them. I make it clear to my customers that they should take a half on their first try unless they want to risk the reaction I had. If they do have a problem I don't want to hear about it.

I'm living life as a sober boy consumed with Playboy magazines. On my rounds around base doing fire inspections I keep a sharp eye out for porn or whatever passes for it. Copies of Playboy are understood to be owned by whoever is holding them.

1/15 Mail Call...James Krasowski

Pete,

I received your season greeting – thanks. I've been receiving a lot of mail lately from everyone under the sun – I must admit, I didn't expect some of the letters, - so with that under consideration- plus the fact that I've been quite busy with my studies –please excuse my belated reply.

I really enjoyed the holidays here – although sometimes the Christmas away from home syndrome got a hold of me. The Germans celebrate Christmas much more simply than we do – and in so doing, the Christmas is much less commercial than ours. The end result of course is that this Christmas can not only be appreciated more but somehow one gets the feeling that "this is the way it should be". The German New Years Eve is celebrated vigorously – more fireworks are used that night than we use on the fourth of July – again the scene was one of beauty and excitement, as well as "fairy tale" in nature. All in all, I enjoyed New Year's more –drinking my Weisiwein (white wine) and smoking a few bowls – mellow.

Michael wrote a letter from Nam – he seems to be coming along pretty good. He's off the front line and

he only has 80 fucking days left in this green machine.
Wow I really didn't think he was that short! Well
anyhow, he accepted my invitation to travel the States
this summer with me and your brother but I wrote
back explaining that now that I'm in Europe, I think I'll
stick to Europe in travel –I'm awaiting a reply. I could
really dig the idea of Michael and/or your brother
tripping Europe with me.

Bob Provoost wrote a few weeks ago- they seem to
be delaying any proceedings against him – I wrote
him a few suggestions and offered some financial
assistance – I hope he comes through this bust alright.
Bob being in Italy, I've decided that I'll probably trip
down and say hello to him either in April or after I get
out in June.

I don't know whether I informed you or not but the 95
gram Christmas present I sent to your brother got
through beautifully - that could mean at least $350 for
my European out – it will also keep your brother
financially secure for months to come. Anna wrote

mentioning that Michael also sent something to Tom – and it got through! Your brother is probably carrying a lot of shit around lately.

The only other news here is the fact that I still have 140 days to go. Oh one question – will you be able to receive any mail after February? If not – wow – dig it - I really hope your head stays right where it is now – have fun, if possible –enjoy what nature has supplied to your head –and until I'm able to rap to you again – Pete –stay mellow

Peace your bro, Jim

"Build the things that war will destroy and I'll come to scavenge afterwards." The Scavengers.

In Laos, the U.S. funded invasion featuring the best of the ARVN stalls as a rainy Boy Scout jamboree. Everyone wants to go home except the enemy. Nightly mortar attacks keep the visiting team awake and a slow death by cuts makes sitting still ill-advised.

The ARVN fights the NVA at Tchephone. With his troops clinging to the skids of evacuating helicopters an ARVN senior officer declares victory. Back across the Uncle Ho toll road he reports the enemy crushed and their resources drained.

Our President announces that "Vietnamization" means an end to us doing all the work.

1/16. Zoomie comes back to the firehouse from the Playboy Hut. He pukes before crashing in Arfy's rack. He's too cute to get written up.

1/18. I sell some more pills to an insistent Coastie. These guys are leaving town so they don't care about what trouble they might get me in. If one of them pulls the nightmare trip that I did they'll be blabbing to the fleet. I warn them to be careful, after I get paid.

1/21. At morning muster the Chief is enraged. When a black guy turns red you know he's pissed. Homer stands beside the Chief with his head bowed and a bloody scab on his nose.

"Gentlemen, I'm pissed and I'm going to stay pissed till the day I leave here. Don't even think about fucking up like Hall. This man was stupid enough to say to me, 'I never thought I'd be working for nigger.'

"I could take a stripe for that remark but I went in another direction. Hall better appreciate that. I've accepted his apology but if I hear even one racial joke, I don't give a fuck how funny you think you are I'll make our time here miserable."

The incident took place in the EM Club. Homer was shit-faced and probably did it on a bet. He might have gotten thrown off the ice for the stunt. Hall's a gambler; rumor has it he once won $3,000 playing dice at a shipyard. He called an ambulance to get himself out of the game; he knew the other players weren't going to let him leave.

Gambling on the ice is a nightly affair fueled by hard drink. Fortunes change hands and then change back. Homer may have lost a bet with a redneck. After chow we fight a fire in the cosmic ray hut, a welcome break from in-house tension.

At Hut Point we see seals swim past. Zoomie tips a forklift into a ditch outside town. The Chief and I go out on foot. I don't think the Chief wants the whole base to know about another fuck up on his watch.

1/25. The tourist ship Lindblad Explorer calls McMurdo. The ship sits in the sound and a flying wedge of civilians come ashore via water taxi. Some guys hide; they don't want to break a streak of not seeing a woman for a year. No such restraint from the fire department. We take every chance we can to ogle one blonde and a few runner-ups. I hear that upon leaving a party at the Chief's Club one of the female visitors grabbed the inside door handle which is shaped as a dildo. With it still in her hand the place broke into applause and the woman into tears. This was told to me, I don't care if it's true; I love bullshit.

American deaths in Vietnam average 100 a week. At McMurdo we lose not a soul. We're in the right place at the right time. Dudes who could be us are missing body parts. Hunkered down here, we're not subject to friendly fire or a booby trap. Our sick bay handles hemorrhoids and vasectomies.

1/27. John, Britain and I go to Automotive to smoke pot with Caskey. John passes out from holding a hit down too long. Mitch walks in while John is out and insists on an explanation. I tell him John slipped into a deep trance related to his Meher Baba meditations. Mitch doesn't buy it. After John wakes we go to mid-rats. A polar bear cub wrestling his brother on an ice floe is a thousand piece jigsaw left on a card table in the lounge; only the border is in place.

1/29.The supply ship USS Towle is in town and I'm assigned to the storekeeper crew working at a pass above town. We're stacking lube oil barrels. A line of forklifts carry the barrels up to the pass, suspended from their blades. We build stacks of fifteen in the shape of racked pool balls. I'm climbing the sides of the triangle stacks guiding the barrels into place and unclamping the lifting straps. Two barrels converge on my finger and turn the nail black. My arm starts to swell. Over at the dispensary they burn a hole in my fingernail using a heated paper clip. I get a splint and a bandage. The corpsmen love this kind of stuff. They might be patching Marines in the jungle if USARP hadn't called. I'm not so damaged I can't return to work.

1/31. Old Boats and I extinguish a burning electrical connection underneath the dispensary then swagger back to the firehouse with our Ansul bottles muzzle down. We have put out the fire on foot.

2/1. When the real cold comes, it brings its bags. The Towle sits alongside the McMurdo pier. The onboard booms set cargo ashore. Frank and I are in a pier crew charged with unhooking the lifting cables. It's -35F and blowing nonstop. Between loads we put our heads down and plod back to a heated shack too small to sit down in. We are learning to love the indoors. At chow I run into Robinson, he's been sent back from Beardmore. We shoot pool at the fire house.

2/2. Another day up in the pass building oil drum pyramids. We're building them close as cars in a dealer's lot. Britain gets in a shouting match with Mr. Smith. While on fire patrol, I find a January 71 Playboy, the first issue to show the centerfold's pubic hair. Liv Lindeland, with one knee raised, reveals her pea patch, the garden Butch insists we cultivate. Bernie agrees to take my overnight watch. I'm exhausted from working outdoors. I go to bed with Miss Lindeland, guilty when I think of Cynthia.

2/3. My role in unloading the Towle is on hold. I'm a towel holder, in a base scrub up. At the dump, I wing a rock at a skua gull enthroned at the buffet table. The rock hits her in the head and she doesn't fly away No one kills the bird population here; this pretty girl doesn't possess the reflex to fly away. Perhaps I'm the first person who has ever thrown anything at her. At 21, I possess an impulse toward indiscriminate massacre. I could be a war criminal if my orders were My Lai. The crimes of 1968 are being investigated in 1971. We're out of earshot for Lt. Calley's testimony but even from the smell of the USO newsletters the deal is absurd. Can one man account for a massacre?

I pass Kees' rack. It's made up to boot camp standards. Everything down to the folded facecloth is in place. Someone tapes a giant X of masking tape across his rack. When confronted, I blame Frank.

"You know he calls himself - Tape Man. He's serious about it. Frank is losing orbit."

The same stuff gets pulled on me. Shampoo drops on Cynthia's breasts – innocent enough –an Ansul canister in my rack, very funny. Anything that makes the day pass faster is welcome. Cheating at cards is understood, we are a far away Navy playing penny poker.

2/5. Zone inspection means cleaning up inside and out. During lunch we smoke hash in Marty's room.

Laine and I throw a Frisbee around until Mr. Flick arrives. He marks our workplace outstanding. There are Airdale stag flicks after our nightly feature.

We don't frag at McMurdo. Mickey Mouse regulations are overlooked unless you're making yourself a pain in the ass. We're in the Navy; you can't act like anything goes, just because we're on the ice. Cmdr Maddox bursts into the radio station to chew Fang's ass over saying "Fuck" on the base radio station. There's a line that shouldn't be cussed. Russ Peterman has to walk our enraged C.O. back to his quarters. Fang wonders if he'll lose stripe. If the Old Man is pissed enough he might start enforcing some rules. We don't salute officers down here. The haircut rules are being dodged. Fang is not the only guy to fuck up. Tom Chambers fuels the Admin Jeep with diesel which puts it out of commission for over a month. I have no stripes to lose. I swagger on my fire patrol.

The last hour of my watch lasts as long as the first three. When I get up and tap the wall clock to insure its working I'm ready to be relieved. I don't go anywhere near my rack which is splayed open as a waiting lover. Chances are I've run out of things to do. When waking my relief I don't cut corners. It takes two people to muck up a shift change.

"Say 'I'm awake'."

"Will you tell me what I want to hear?'

"You're shorter by a day."

When you wake your mate, insure he's fully conscious. You can't just shake his shoulder and walk away. Your last entry in the log should mention his name.

"Okay I'm up, hit your rack. Remind me of our mission?"

"Eat, drink, sleep."

2/7. Sunday we hold a movie matinee. After a morning field day, we watch <u>Far From the Madding Crowd</u> and discuss what we would do if we found ourselves alone with Julie Christie. Kees adds dialogue

Hardy would hardly approve. It is about the seventh time this flick has been our main attraction. After a steak lunch we're back in the firehouse watching Nobody's Perfect. I'm playing casino with Boats when Zoomie comes in the house stinking drunk. He sets his rack on fire with a cigarette. Second time this week we fight a fire without using a fire truck.

Days are as repetitious as the entries in our log. The stacked sentences in this handwriting sampler inspire me to ad-lib. I try to include weather conditions, the color of the sky and present temperature. I've been lectured about the integrity of a Navy log so I won't write anything that can't be defended. I include a countdown to the September win fly.

Mr. Apollinaire's heroic Prince Vibescu is a rich kid in a self-published uniform. To escape the buggering of a senior self-appointed officer he flees to Paris. There he swears to two whores that he will bring them twenty orgasms or die the death of a thousand cuts.

This playful tale celebrates an author trysting with words wearing lingerie. The blood-racing plot allows the light-headed reader to catch his breath between chapters. It's a strong cheese, meant to be eaten in the dead of winter.

Mr. Apollinaire portrays his hero as a ladies' man with a sizeable inheritance whose only interest is sex. In an effort to shock the reader his hero delights in taking it in his butt. I'm reading this on the ice. Mony does more than enough pleasuring with woman of all ages to insure this is not a gay novel. You would have to take a day off to imagine some perversion not covered in this 121 page stroke book of genius.

2/9. We're back to ship unloading. The USS Wyandot is in port. Frank and I work the pier all morning and MacKay works with me in the afternoon. We use volcanic dust to spell out a giant Fuck You on the snow covered pier. The onboard boatswain mate gets the message and flips us the bird. Skids of Budweiser and Schlitz fly over the side and onto the pier. There is a small inventory of Antarctica beer which no one drinks. It's souvenir beer. I drink one Bud as a nightcap and suffer an occasional Schlitz because Cynthia Meyers is their spokes girl.

2/13. The Wyandot has to turn around and put its starboard side against the pier. It takes all day and ends with crushed pilings. I'm assigned to assist a First Class Quartermaster named Ming who has been sent down to test drive a Mike boat. It's an open inboard with a three step ladder down to its engine compartment. The Wyandot has set the boat down alongside itself like a bath toy. I'm aboard to pass down parts, hold the flashlight and stand watch topside. Ming goes below to fiddle with firing cartridges. After a long hour the boat comes to life. We putt putt at a half knot, the boat choking on cold water.

I'm on the same sound that hosted the Endurance, the Aurora, the Discovery and my favorite exploring ship the Nimrod. I'm picturing men driven mad by famine plodding toward us harnessed as sled dogs. We're fifty yards offshore and solemn as a fishing charter. I'm second in command on my very first sea duty. Inside my head I keep an eye on chow hours. You must eat well if you work outdoors. Ming exudes a mood for no questions. We're not moving forward or back. I see Ming later that night. He's exiting the EM club. He's drunk and doesn't recognize me. His mission is over, his boat has failed.

When you sleep in under-heated quarters, your body tenses up instead of relaxes. Curled under covers you try to create a pool of body heat. It's hard to get to sleep and when you do, you want to kill anyone who wakes you. I hear guys brag of ripping off 12 hour naps as if rehearsing hibernation. Firehouse "nooners" imply a one hour nap. I take a pillow and blanket and sleep under my rack to avoid Arfy's afternoon reveille.

One thing sure to piss my Dad off is me being out in the cold without a hat. He must have experienced some childhood trauma and swore no kid of his would ever go lidless. My brother Tom and I were too cool to wear hats when we were kids. After you outgrow your Davy Crockett there are no cool hats. At McMurdo your cover is an essential piece of your uniform. I've been sent home from the Nuke plant alarm and threatened with being written up by a Chief who caught me hatless at the dump. I usually wear a green field cap without the Elmer Fudd earflaps but I often misplace it or it gets blown off. You have to pull a knife on Dale Myers to get him to issue you a new one.

2/11. I get a package from my brother Tom. A paperback edition of Lord of the Flies, hollowed out with a Xacto knife. It is done with a level of precision that allows a square of hash to rest inside with no trace of it showing when the book is closed. Suddenly I have something that no one else in my world has. Krasowski has sent it to my brother and my brother has sent it to me. It's a block that's been stepped on in four continents.

A squad of stoners creates a four hose hookah from an empty wine bottle, rubber stoppers, glass tubes and hoses. We pack a bowl and start puffing. After two turns, the circle relaxes into a consensus. "We can make it through the winter."

The end of the workday holds a reward for juicers – beer or booze. For a small circle of friends converging at the firehouse there's a peace pipe and a Poco album.

2/15. John isn't doing pills after the event with the Poison. I'm in no hurry to get that high again. I give Andy some of the Poison and he says they don't get him high. I won't argue - I love bullshit. With summer about to end, I have two dozen hits of THC, some mescaline and a hash snack the size of a moon pie. At the radio station I play "Baby You're a Rich Man."

2/16. Kees and I go to our PACE correspondence class (History 101) where a video teacher walks us through a workbook. It kills the morning and is more fun than wire brushing Ansul bottles. In the afternoon we take a class in Philosophy.

Kees goes to the club and comes back drunk. We start teasing him, calling the Navasota a Coast Guard reserve mike boat. He's too drunk to get enraged. You don't rank on a sailor about his ship – he can disparage it, you shouldn't. Worry about your own sorry ass existence. Kees goes face down in his bunk. We stand by expecting puke.

He's conflicted. He's knows I have this hash but he's not going to participate in any smoking club. We fire up in the second class quarters with a lookout at the door. We will move the party to the second deck or smoke at Stores to keep Kees from having to avert his eyes. It's too cold to go outside. No hard feelings from me; Kees and I review Philosophy.

"Nobody cares what you think," my Mom would say if I suggested any type of philosophy. "No one asked you anything. Why would the world be curious about what you're thinking? Zip your lip- do some listening - shut your trap." It's her philosophy.

The words are not exact but the message had an effect. If you're talking to me let's talk about you. I don't consider myself an authority on any subject. I'm surrounded by older guys with more experience at being around other guys. A few of the firehouse crew are my age but most of this base is older than me by years or decades. Being the lowest enlisted man in town I'm expected to respect the higher ranks around me. Unless I'm being ordered to get a haircut, I'll do what I'm told. I have no authority over anyone else; it emboldens me to act as I do. Old Boats leaves the ice. He's fighting to stay in the Navy.

2/19. Les is in from Byrd. We smoke a toast to his arrival. Les brought the first pot I ever smoked into our Davisville barracks concealed inside stereo speakers. His trail goes Rantoul-Da Nang-McMurdo. He could make a living on the mound in fast pitch softball. The hash through a water pipe smells like eggnog. I cut strips off the block with a pocket knife. Les fills us in on the close quarters at Byrd. McMurdo is as spacious as a federal pen.

2/20. We smoke at the firehouse and then go to Fang's room. Some powerful grass is passed around and I realize that I have no business being behind the wheel. Then I remember I'm not driving. Out in the street I puke three times. I crash in my rack from over-smoking. Thank God we don't get any real alarms.

2/21. During watch I walk down to the harbor and perch. The summer is disappearing. I'm enjoying the day night while I can. The short-timers are partying like crazy and I'm in the middle of it. Across the anonymous icescape winter waits on a train.

2/22. I go to 155 and take what's called a Hollywood shower. Living at the firehouse requires attention to grooming. I'm the only guy I know who carries a hairbrush. Pytlik smirks when he sees me getting away with my longer than regulation hair. I suspect he acts as a double agent.

2/23. I write my last letter to Kathy and send a few pictures. From now till September we write Mars-grams or get an occasional phone patch. Mars-grams are typed messages that arrive via teletype. It's a love letter you get after eight other guys have read it.

2/24. Outside the firehouse I see a penguin running by like a man trying to catch a bus. When his momentum overcomes him, he body surfs on his belly. Behind him comes a line of stragglers. Mr. Pruitt picks one up and cradles it like a new born. Frank, Homer and I kidnap the little guy and bring him into the EM club. He stands on the bar to get his picture taken. That night on watch I wander down to the shore where the seals lay out like cigars in a box. I'm tired enough to consider snuggling in with them.

2/26. Today was the last flight out and it took Zoomie home. We sat with our fingers crossed praying he would make the plane. The door is shut on 160 guys waiting for dark. Kees and Andy drive the Old Man's jeep back from Willie field. Andy moves into the second class quarters. I have no idea why but evening chow is served by candlelight. We're hosting Kiwis.

2/28. I have taken over Zoomie's abandoned rack and expanded the stoner zone that is my end of our sleeping quarters. I have a Jimi Hendrix poster, a Bob Dylan poster and Cynthia Meyers under glass. Andy hooked something up so the music from my stereo plays in his room below. After evening chow, Tim, Andy and I each take a hit of THC, smoke some hash and ride inner tubes down Suicide Hill. Near freeze my ass off.

When Shackleton was here there was a war going on that he knew nothing about. He left for the ice while WW1 was in warm ups. Sledding around down here he had no idea about what was going on up there. The only Englishmen not following the conflict were Ernie and his mates.

Antarctica makes you snow blind to the north. It is the globe's great hideout, put your feet up, grow a beard, fast, take a vow of silence, ship over, get your balls nipped, read a book a second time, sand a shamrock tat off your calf, bullshit, ping pong, pool, cards, shut the fuck up, eat, drink and be contrary. We are not of Shackleton stock. Our only bond is ignorance of the war.

I write phony news releases to read between records.

Dateline Cam Ran Bay March 1971 – U. S. ground forces have been joined by the first sight impaired platoon in Vietnam. Every man under the command of Lieutenant Keller had been judged unsuitable for service. Due to his enthusiasm and determination he has convinced the brass that his men are just as able to hunt down and engage the enemy as our existing units. They expect to not see action in Al Dak province.

3/1. New firehouse rules – no reveille on Sunday, longer nooners.

3/3. Homer calls us into his quarters, one at a time, to talk about drugs. This is a requirement for his career path toward Chief. Everyone knows he's bucking for it but has been passed over due to his weight. I've left my stash with John to hide in 155. I might have the only recreational pills and hash at McMurdo. I'm obliged to protect them.

The Navy opened the base at McMurdo in 1955. Every man assigned here after that has been a bigger pussy than the guy he relieved. Every year McMurdo gets bigger, better, softer, more attractive - evolving into an Anchorage Econolodge. In the 1971 firehouse, we man an outpost across the street from everybody else except the crazy USARPS who live in shacks on the outskirts of town. One has a door spray-painted orange.

Cynical as infantry we pursue assignments that make no sense. We do as little work as possible to avoid running out of work altogether. Give me a paintbrush and I'll see you at lunch. In the Navy - "If you can piss you can paint". The man who enjoys his own company has the required Zen to work unsupervised. Indoors,

I'm apt to apply myself. Outdoors whatever I'm doing I'm doing fast. The cold puts a foot in your ass.

In chapter 2 Apollinaire's hero is at an orgy interrupted by bandits. The intruders bind up the Prince and he watches his playmates get ravished by a duo that would have been happy just to steal his watch. His girlfriends are forced to whip him. The party ends with a member bitten off and a dagger into the taint of a harlot. Months of rest are required for the Prince's flagellation wounds to heal. The Prince experiences pain as pleasure. A maid at his hotel is his mistress during recovery.

3/4. I get a haircut. I can't stand sneaking around avoiding Chiefs. Pytlik gives me a knowing smile.

"I heard that Homer was catching shit about you from lifers at the club."

Homer's my boss and he wants to be a Chief. I don't want to embarrass him. Pytlik tones me down to a less offensive length without going whitewall. This will be my last haircut on this tour. Fang laughs at my hair at chow – I want to kill him.

3/8. Roger bakes hash brownies.

3/9. Quarterly marks with Mr. Elkins - mine are poor. My suitability for promotion is low. Stars start appearing on a darkening sky. A new haircut policy is announced – you don't have to cut it until it's time to go home-Great, if I held off for two days I could have gone a year without a haircut.

3/11. Andy moves his rack upstairs along with his posters and black light. We now have a look of an opium den. Andy has the overnight watch. We can't get inspired to go outdoors it's -45F.

3/12. The package store opens and we all buy wine. During the movie Duffy, the bottles pass around. When the lights come on Andy, Kees, Ed and Homer are wrecked. Andy crashes then gets up to puke. Conrad smacks a fire truck into an Ansul sled and he's the only one sober.

George Kunzweiler is a Second Class Quartermaster who volunteered for Vietnam. He says he was sick and tired of guys talking about "the shit". There's no more broke dick post than barracks cleaner at Pensacola.

In Nam, George is assigned to Pysch-Ops – appropriate for a guy who volunteers. He winds up on a walking tour of villages with a boom box tied to his back, blasting a funeral dirge meant to make cadres homesick. Twenty five hundred men answer his siren call.

"That many less shooting at us," he suggests.

If it's bullshit, we're happy to hear it. We're encouraged the Navy is doing more than shelling from offshore.

George claims the North Vietnamese are smarter than us and the South Vietnamese are smarter than them. No one on our side speaks the native language. Enlisted men know we are getting played. The ARVN during the day is the VC at night. Everybody is getting paid. When George's tour is over he asks for orders to somewhere not so hot. He winds up wintering over and driving us crazy with the word "bokoo".

3/18. Someone put grease on my hairbrush. It's a joke, I get it but you can't buy a hairbrush like this down here. I love a prank but it shouldn't destroy personal property. I suspect Arfy dreamt this up and just overdid it. He has a Baby Huey enthusiasm about himself and how he fits in at the firehouse. On duty he apologizes for asking you to do anything. I have a phone patch with Kathy. I resist the temptation to complain about my hairbrush. I don't want her to think I'm crazy.

3/19. I have six sisters so I've been around people on the rag. Today everybody seems to be picking on me. I retreat to my rack after field day reading The Mask of Fu Manchu. I have no way of brushing my hair.

3/20. We're painting the radio station. After work I drink some wine with Homer in his room. We're not going to agree on hash but I respect the man and ask him to sit for an interview for the base newspaper. Tim Groshen and I shoot pool. I propose an idea of using bamboo strips to frame the walls of the radio station.

3/22. Tonight's movie is The Bliss of Mrs. Blossom.

3/25. We play Hell instead of poker.

Meher Baba kept a vow of silence for thirteen years. He would've been a blast on the ice. He walked around with a hand-held blackboard on which he spelled out messages with magnetic letters. His small-press pamphlets entitled Discourses get passed around by his devotees while they await their turn to read his bio I AM GOD –in the mirror DOGMA 1. John offers me a pamphlet, as a break from Apollinaire. When Frank sees me reading it he asks in dead earnest –"Does Meher Baba jerk off?" I find no mention of masturbation in his text so I assure Frank that he does and doesn't talk about it. Baba is a God and a regular guy.

Guys living in close proximity need to synchronize the talking listening dynamic. I don't want you to mope around like Laine but at the same time, Zoomie, shut the fuck up. Strive to land between chatter and chatter-box. When two or more guys are within six feet of each other someone has got to carry the ball. Make sure it's not always the same guy. Killing the day is everybody's job. This is where bullshit asserts itself. If you dream up a story that requires days of debate to disprove, you've done a public good. I floated the rumor, early in the tour that Miss Universe was to visit the ice. I take credit for the claim that reading Meher Baba's opus results in tantric sexual release. I insist that people have told me that reading the guru opens you to a force as forceful as a nocturnal emission. I've never read Baba's book. There are only two copies in town. It is 600 pages long with no pictures.

3/27. Our basketball court is an unheated Quonset hut. I'm assigned to a crew charged with nailing plywood to the walls to block out the wind. I'm the only one who shows up and instead of standing around freezing I flip the sheets up and start nailing them over the most serious drafts.

Mr. Flick calls me to his room and chews my ass. I'm distracted by his Baba lapel pin. Some Seabees have complained to him that my half-ass job might be credited to them. I tell Mr. Flick I didn't think we were building the Taj Mahal and I was trying to stay warm. He makes me promise to never pick up a hammer outside of the firehouse.

In the spring of 1971 more people are protesting the war than fighting it. In our corner of the globe no one talks foreign policy. We are here to support scientific research and clean up after ourselves. Dozens of countries have signed the Antarctic Treaty and observe its rules without incident. Every other continent seems to need a time out.

Mr. Apollinaire was a French art critic and avant garde poet high on opium and absinthe. He invented the term "surrealism" and created a library of distinguished work that does not include The Debauched Hoposdar. It was a work commissioned by a rich patron who wanted a novel that would amuse his mistress. It is claimed that any woman who reads the book finishes it with her legs thrown open.

One of Mony's conquests is Culculine d'Ancone, a nineteen year old beauty he meets on the street.

"I've squeezed dry the purses of nineteen millionaires," she agrees to have Mony take her arm.

It's so quiet I hear the snap of a jigsaw. I lie beside a book of completed crosswords. There's a sixty mile an hour wind ripping through town and no reason for going outdoors. Hunkered down as our mates in Nam - we reflect a hundred degree swing in temperature. We know less about the war than the guys fighting it and they know less than the people watching it on TV. There are 160 of us here and 500,000 guys over there.

Safe and not warm on the frozen front – we're as rear echelon as any senator's son.

3/26. Zone inspection; Andy finishes remodeling his rack while everyone else does field day. At 1330 we pass and secure for the day. At 1930 Andy and I drop mescaline. Fang comes over and we talk while a rush comes over me like a back rub for my brain. Fast Eddie is drinking Jim Beam and getting lost in the middle of a story. We are laughing so hard, the people watching the movie complain. Ed crashes in his rack. Andy and I stay up to 0500. I fall out. Andy is on duty to 0700.

It is 1971 and we are ready to get out of Vietnam. The search and destroy days are on hold. We're waiting for the ARVN to step forward.

"You can't beat a dog to make it hunt." Read this in a book.

3/27. Andy sleeps in because he had night watch. John comes over and for the second day in a row I take pills. One hit of THC and a half of mescaline. Andy wakes up and takes a half hit of the Poison. Far from the Madding Crowd is playing again and I sit strapped to my chair. My circle of bearded comrades stays up talking, laughing and listening to albums. Among this poor man's Paris artist colony, I indulge my ambition to write a porno novel.

The title is Cheese Filled Buns and the story details the sex adventures of Archie, an Entenmanns's Bakery delivery man. Of course I'm imitating Apollinaire while not stealing anything word for word. I resolve to answer the Hospodar's invitation to derangement with a sense of comedy. The sex in my story is eye to eye with nothing kinkier than a spiked heel in a cheesecake. Guillaume was a poet – that's the recipe for a sick sex life. I'm a sailor - the sensualist hero of every sea story.

In my first chapter Archie drives his route accompanied by a couple, intent on making love in a box truck of pastry. He does the play by play through his rear view mirror.

My audience provides polite encouragement. Smoking comes first and then the reading. The critics in my room sit in powwow till the start of mid-rats. Conversation is local bullshit and rock and roll trivia. Stoned out threads of magical thinking are sliced into laughing fits. We don't talk about home or the war we're sitting out. Crossing from the firehouse to 155 in a -50F wind storm testifies to the pull of the midnight snack.

03/28. I empty the shitter and Andy and I switch out the piss barrel. After mid-rats we go to the radio station for my 0300-0700 radio show. We smoke hash and drink cold Cokes. I plug in a hot plate that knocks my show off the air.

I take a deep inhale of homesickness. My brother Artie and my sister Mary Lou are in the Army. She's in Massachusetts, he's in Germany. Tom has Jesus length hair and a map of Canada. My parents must be going crazy. Mom promised to write to me every day even when we don't get mail. I imagine her letters piling up at the ChiChi mail depot. I'll have to read them in chronological order when they arrive on the winfly.

When Fang smiles his teeth reach out to grab you around the neck. He had his nickname long before I met him. His goofy look suggests a central casting sidekick. At Davisville we would watch him play softball. Les pitched so effectively that his fielders got bed sores. One towering fly descended so slow Fang could have tied his shoe while waiting for it. When he caught it, we whistled and stomped our feet to break his balls. He shot us the finger in front of a grandstand of families. The manager pulled him out of the game. At McMurdo he is the assistant editor of our winter over newspaper, the Super Sunday Sometimes.

3/28. The first edition of the Super Sunday Sometimes rolls off the mimeograph and into the chow hall. Borrowing from Playboy, I contribute an in depth interview with a man about town. In a base this size everybody doesn't know everybody else. My first subject is "Big Mac" (Laundry Man) Dave McCracken.

3/28.   Super Sunday Sometimes

Interview with Dave McCracken

Mac is picking at his evening chow as we begin. He's wearing his trademark bandanna and Norton undershirt. His slow chewing cheeks mimic a restless sleeper.

SSS: Big Mac, you seem to have snapped out of a week-long funk –what turned the Tide?

Mac: It wasn't stupid detergent jokes.

SSS: Dave, we're ALL happy to see you in good CHEER. We WISK you all the best.

Mac: Really, this is an interview?

SSS: What about the slow eating – have you always been this way?

Mac: I'm the only Ships Serviceman who does laundry. Unless Kees comes over to help, I spend my days with dirty clothes. Don't get on my case about how I eat.

SSS: You do the USARPS laundry?

Mac: That's confidential. You want to talk about skivvies talk about your own.

SSS: What type of stuff goes on in your shop that might interest our readers?

Mac: That time you burned you neck while riding in the dryer.

SSS: Other than that.

Mac: The other day I found a funny cigarette in a shirt pocket.

SSS: Quick bring it here.

Mac: I gave it to Chief Z.

SSS: You grew up in Lancaster Pa. What's it like living between Brandywine and Intercourse?

Mac: You're doing road map jokes? I grew up on a farm. We had chickens. My Dad wouldn't let me have a dog because he was afraid it would kill the chickens. Do you know what kind of pet I had?

SSS: A cat?

Mac: A chicken. A black chicken named Elvis because Dad thought Elvis was black until he saw him on TV.

SSS: A chicken won't fetch a stick.

Mac: No kidding. That chicken would stand in the yard pecking feed. After every peck he would turn his head in a circle with as many stops as the second hand on a pocket watch. The other chickens got fat but not Elvis. Nobody wants a skinny chicken.

SSS: Hold on - I think we've made a breakthrough.

Dave ends the interview. He takes his Jell-O back to his room. He may still be eating it by the time you read this.

3/29. Homer's Heroes vs. Waldo's Warriors headlines the card at our two lane bowling alley. We use a human pinsetter. I bowl 94,108 and 110. This kind of detail helps fill my diary. I've taken to writing in larger script to fill up one page. Homer helps me file my income tax.

Cheese Filled Buns revolves around Archie's attraction to women's asses. No other body part holds his interest to this degree. Delivering glazed pastries curved as derrieres leaves him in heat. Chapter 2 involves Archie's call on a flirty fifty year old housewife sitting on her kitchen counter, housedress raised as the colors. After a turn of snappy dialogue, Archie's hand closes over her sticky éclair. Cut to Chapter Three. A few guys in my round table admit to staying awake. Others ask if I could play an album.

4/1. SSS Editor's note: A manuscript has been found on the doorstep of our favorite newspaper. It purports to be the diary of Doctor Carl Dish - a firsthand account of his disappearance from Longwire Station on May, 8 1965. How it was written and how it reached us are issues currently under investigation. In the meantime we will share some excerpts with our readers. We have space to fill.

From the Diary of Doctor Dish

There's a germ in my brain that makes me want to be alone. I hated my parents for making me play with other kids. Once my Mother pushed me out the door screaming "Go make some godamn friends" We were both crying. I stood around watching other kids with names like Matt Howard and Billy Baker. When it was time to go home I ran all the way. I'm paraphrasing a German poet – "We are blind until we see we are unspeakably alone."

There was a girl named Arlene Tryme. I would watch her chip away at a bologna sandwich with the precision of a chain saw sculptor. When I had the nerve to sit at her table I was stupid enough to ask "Is Tryme your real name?" She got up from the table in tears. Imagine me commenting on someone's name.

To be continued next week.

4/2. A shooting star in the western sky could be incoming. High as I am, I imagine the echo pop of distant artillery. The guys I'm with go inside to eat. I don't want to go inside; my head hits the ceiling. Alone at the ice shelf, my spirit lifts as a falcon off my forearm. It sweeps across the sky figure skating crazy eights. I'm toasted on a half tab of mescaline and a bowl of hash. Aurora australis spray paints the sky like a Queens's subway car. I light a firecracker beside Arfy's rack as payback for my hairbrush. There is less light in each new day.

I'm in a mood to hug the world. My short-time on the sober is over. I'm using THC. This is not a narcotic; this is not an addictive drug, it's not even hallucinogenic most of the time. It's God putting his arm across your shoulder. Under the influence of this pill, I watch the sky birth stars. Back in my rack, hallucinations shuffle the overhead. Paisley amoeba slow dance to Brewer and Shipley side two.

4/3. Chief Baker visits the firehouse doused in drink. In respect to his rank we make him a place at our poker game. He eats the first card dealt to him. Frank, Ed and I go to lift weights; try to make that sound interesting.

4/6. We draw down musical instruments from Special Services. A trumpet for Fast Eddie, a guitar for Frank and I get a Catalina. We give one concert before musical instruments are banned from the firehouse. An alarm sounds at the Bio Lab; I arrive on the back of the La France without a hat. Our C.O. threatens to write me up if he ever catches me uncovered. He won't bust me this time; his warning is issued at a false alarm. Kees gets his ear pierced.

4/7 Movie Marathon features <u>In Cold Blood</u> and <u>Barbarella.</u>

An April Fools story is now a weekly series for SSS. Roger Turner and I will take turns providing Doctor's Dish's field notes.

4/11   The Super Sunday Sometimes

              From the Diary of Doctor Dish

My departure from Longwire will mark the end of colonialism in Antarctica. I intend to negotiate with only those who accept me as a sovereign nation. I haven't yet conceived of a flag but I have plenty of time to think. Above life, I prize self-determination. I call myself Ho Chi Minus-50F.

As a microbiologist I have access to supplies ordered on the most casual pretense. Summer mail drops have carried in steroids and the traditional snacks that served Shackleton, Scott and Amundsen. A series of breathing exercises that would bore you to death have given me the power to control my own metabolism. Mind over body training has enabled me to stroll around Byrd in my birthday suit. If you remember the guy who ascended Everest in his boxer shorts-I'm doing the same kind of training. The magician who put himself inside a block of ice read the same text as me. Glidine mixed with Trumilk is my trail mix. I practice a secret yoga favored by swamis, samurais and Navy Seals

In a cocoon of my own design I'm able to sleep outdoors. As a desert lizard keeps cool by burying itself in the sand, I stay warm as a family room under six inches of snow. My body heat mixed with that of my husky Gus creates an organic electric blanket. I've trained the dog to cuddle despite the cruel remarks of my Navy mates.

"Does she do it human-style?" This is the kind of crack I've learned to deflect. When I bleach the dog's fur pure white, I'm asked to chat with a visiting Chaplain.

"My work is classified," I remind Chaplain Morris. "I'm an agnostic. Is there anything else to discuss?"

"Carl, we want to insure you are sound of mind."

"Chaplain, that's a question you could ask of any man who settles to bottom of the world."

"Carl you're walking around naked."

Gus's sled mates know her smell as well as mine. They are trained to track anyone lost on the ice. A dozen false leads will lead them on a fool's errand. I expect my disappearance will be attributed to a fall into an ice crevasse. My mates will have little appetite for striking out in random directions under winter storm conditions. Most of them couldn't find their way from Byrd to Longwire. My calculations forecast high winds, snowstorms and uninterrupted night. Spotting a white body bag buried in a snow drift approximates finding a sandbox in the Sahara. I know men will risk their lives trying to find me. That is a cost associated with the birth of a nation.

To be continued in next week's issue.

4/12. When I do an overnight radio show I sleep till lunch. On the air I'm jacked as any college DJ; concerned with dead air and dry commentary. I recap who did what in local sports teams and report orders sending real guys to fictional places.

Today I do Roger's "drive time" radio show. I'm writing bits for the Sunday paper, doing philosphy homework and reading USO copy. Gordon Lightfoot sings the songs.

4/13. The sun is gone and we're lit by stars. The cold hits with hammer blows. After a short patrol I come in and my hands are so numb I can't unzip myself, I have to pee, I always have to pee.

4/14. Frank and I are varnishing molding to be installed in the firehouse kitchen. We have to make the most of every chore. Our nooners are as long as double features. I wake to the world I fell asleep in.

4/15. Between weight lifting, basketball, volleyball and bowling there's a way to mark each day as a sport. One activity has no days off. I'm called to account for my insistent hormones. Frank and I grow close with our erotica. Apollinaire's plot has gotten so perverse; I've retreated to the simple pleasure of looking at photos of naked girls.

4/16. Chambers, John, Fang and I smoke hash and listen to records. Dylan, Ochs and Richie Havens all sing against a war raging on the far side of the world. We're not singing along but I turn the volume up when "I Ain't Marching Anymore" is playing.

4/18. My phone patch catches Kathy's Mom. Kathy is out with friends. We chat for a few minutes. Her Mother is thrilled that I called. I enjoy talking to her but I was hoping for Kathy. Her Mom runs a beauty salon in her basement crammed with devices from a science fiction thriller.

4/20. I'm in some intestinal distress that has me hugging my knees to my chest in a cannonball dive. I roll out of my rack at 0200 and go to sick bay certain I've imagined myself into appendicitis. I'm issued a rack and officially admitted. The staff seems reassured by my presence. You're not supposed to get sick down here so I suppose the corpsmen don't always have enough to do. Like firemen they work on calls. I give blood and urine. After a tab of Belladonna I slip into a coma.

4/21. I'm in my sickbay rack all day. I don't even get up to pee which alarms the corpsman. Bizokti screens a movie for a one man audience. Guys from the firehouse stop by to rag on me. John visits as well. In bed all day I have time to review my life, year by year, then flip it over and review it again. I'm reading Master of Falconhurst which provides the one two punch of a stomach ache and a book that it hurts to read.

4/22. Bed ridden on a slow day in a slow world I can't help but think of home. I'm from a family of ten children- I'm third boy ahead of six sisters and a little brother. They are all somewhere doing something. My oldest brother Artie grew up a step apart from me, my brother Tom a half-step away. We shared a room so small we shared a shadow. I spend hours thinking of Kathy and the times I've talked her into taking her clothes off.

I'm served beef broth and tea and a hit of belladonna. My sleep hallucinations include my grandfather standing at the foot of my rack.

In chapter three, Prince Vibescu meets the bandit who stabbed his girlfriend between her legs. By blackmail the man signs on as the Prince's valet and provides whatever Mony desires. Aboard the Orient Express the rocking dining car has the traditional effect on the Prince. He unbuttons his pants and commands his valet, "Spare me this discomfort."

Before the valet un-gloves, two beauties arrive on the scene. Mony seduces a famous actress with clever poems and the applause meter poking through his fly. Under the table she rubs him off with her delicate feet while his valet and her handmaiden trade kisses. Mony tells the girl her eyes "make stars fall".

At this point Apollinaire turns dark. The plot aims to stun the reader's senses. The author insists his reader either put the book down - if he has any shred of human decency - or applaud the evil men can imagine. The chapter takes predictable activity to unpredictable heights. It ends with the Prince and his valet leaping off a moving train. Their crimes are assumed to be the work of Jack the Ripper.

4/26. I'm still in a sick bay time standstill. I've reviewed every step of my life up to now and find no reason to be clutching my gut in this narrow rack. I froze my feet off last night. Taylor issues me another blanket; excellent medical care.

4/27. I'm out of sickbay. Back at the firehouse everyone is unhappy to see me. My appetite has returned so I eat at the mess. After watch I do my overnight radio show.

4/28. Ed and I go to the radio station to watch Andy do his show. Andy and I are at odds about something neither of us can name. He agrees to do my show so I return to the firehouse. Is he doing me a favor because I have the only drugs around? Getting high is no fun without like-minded company. As far as I know, I have the only stash at McMurdo. It's a burden I bear.

4/28 SSS Interviews Homer Hall

Homer is compared to the Little King cartoon. His gumdrop physique makes him easy to identify. I catch him in the firehouse (he's my boss). He's using stick on labels to make checkers into chess pieces.

SSS: Is it okay to call you Chief, since you're only a first-class?

HH: Inside the firehouse I'm Chief. Outside, I'm a Damage Control First Class with 11 years in the world's greatest Navy.

SSS: Have you served in any other Navy?

HH: I've traveled around the world including two stops in Nam. I've seen what other countries call a navy. I don't have to sit in dog shit to know not to step in it- do you?

SS: Easy Homer, we're here to have fun. Tell our readers a little about yourself.

HH: I grew up in a little town so far north in New York State that I could pee into Canada. I was always a fat kid. I observed that every good story has a fat man in it. I became everybody's fat friend and was elected class President in my senior year. As soon as I joined the U.S. Navy I found my calling. I love this organization.

SS: Spoken like a true lifer, Homer. You sing like that you'll make Chief no matter how fat you are.

HH: Every petty officer is obligated to ensure his strikers advance in rank, it doesn't say -"If you feel like it." See me in my office.

SSS: Homer, you don't have an office. Tell our readers what you would change about this command.

HH: More chiefs less officers.

SSS: Boy you're sucking up.

HH: You think? I'm proud to be a lifer. If you don't like the Navy- I say "Get out." It's not for everybody.

SSS: You make a lot of sense.

HH: Don't try kissing my ass – you're not leaving the ice as an E2.

At this point the interview ends and chow begins. Don't get between this man and his evening meal.

4/28. Staring into the honey bag, I see that some mates are bleeding out their ass. Hemorrhoids are epidemic at our sick bay. Minor scrapes and bad hangovers fill out the scorecard. Mine was the only ailment that rated more than an overnight stay. Before Chief Dinsmore discharged me he agreed to do an interview for our Sunday paper. Frank and I resume staining molding for our remodeled kitchen.

4/28.   SSS From the Diary of Doctor Dish

Sastrugi sounds like something to put tomato sauce on. It is the Russian name given to the white swells that mimic frozen chop. These snow dunes straight-armed the early Antarctic explorers. I will listen for their prayers and curses as I retrace their steps and recover their never claimed caches. Grand adventures don't decompose at this latitude.

Halfway through the movie The Invisible Man, I sympathize with the movie's monster. He is a brilliant scientist who needs complete peace and quiet to prefect his formula but his landlady is always finding a pretext to disturb him.

"My work, my work, I need peace to do my work!"

He implores for naught. Rushed into trying his formula on himself he finds he is unable to return from invisible.

Trapped at Byrd with these navy clowns I can't get enough things done. That's why this movie appeals to me when it's shown in our chow hall theatre. A rare night away from my work inspires me to strive even harder toward a secret goal. It leaves me no time for the grab-ass team building between sailors and scientists that the Navy supports. I move to Longwire to be closer to alone – solitude is a greenhouse for truth.

To be continued in next week's issue.

We hear war stories told by semi-eyewitnesses who served in Da Nang or Cam Ram Bay. George Kunzweiler tells this one more than once.

"I heard a marine tell a story of escorting a wounded man to the rear. They meet a village girl. The marine stomps down a plot of grass for the girl to lie down on. The wounded man holds the girls umbrella over the copulating couple. It's pouring rain. When it's over the wounded man asks the marine how he could rape the girl.

"I told him. I didn't rape her, I paid her. She didn't want to do it but she took the money. Next time hold the umbrella lower, I can't screw with rain in my ass."

George swears it's true as he overheard it. I nod my head –bullshit.

4/29. Homer gets drunk and the Kiwis have to carry him back to his rack.

4/30. I shoot enough eight ball to earn a merit badge. It creates a twitch in my hip from trying to break the rack so that every ball touches a rail. Depending on my partner I can hold the table from 1500 until evening chow. After the movie, stoners form a circle around the pipe. We make a token attempt at being discreet that stops at any thought of going outside. It's -40F. The hawk chills the fillings in my teeth. Today is Frank's birthday. I give him a gift of black licorice.

Whatever happened after that preceded the next thing. The day unreels in real time. When I'm on watch I don't look at the clock. We are certain to be here for the rest of today. Homesickness chokes me. I have to remind myself, I could be in Nam.

Andy tells a story about missing a sailing. He's written up and the paperwork is sitting on the desk of his XO. When the officer steps out of the room Anderson finds his report and slides it between a filing cabinet and the wall.

The XO calls his Yeoman in to find the file. After a futile search he tells Andy to wait outside. Anderson swears he never heard another word about it. I doubt this tale escaped embellishment - bullshit thrives in this climate.

5/1. Fast Eddie is typing paperwork for Homer. Kees took a shot at this job and so did I. Frank and I are still varnishing woodwork and watching stain dry. After evening chow I get stoned with Fang, Mike, Tim, Mac and Chambers.

Gil Mumma wears his hair long but is clean shaven. He's holding court at a table in the mess hall. I'm listening in though he's telling the story to other guys.

"I'm stationed at Point Sur and I've never been to San Francisco. I borrow a buddy's Harley and head south. I'm reading a map at a gas station rest area when a kid walks up and puts a gun to my head."

"Get off the bike."

"The first thought that crosses my mind - Is this helmet bullet proof?"

"The kid's hand is shaking so bad, I turn the gun away and grab his throat. He drops his starter pistol and we begin a two man saloon brawl in a gravel parking lot. I hope it was the toughest fight I'll ever be in. I would've given up a Triumph but you battle for a Harley. My buddy who owned the bike is twice the size of the kid who tried to steal it. He would have killed me if I came back to base on the bus - so much for the summer of love."

As the table sits back to digest that tale, he starts another.

"Same duty station, I'm moonlighting at a service center. I get a call to tow a car gone off the road on a mountain curve. When I get there I find out the girl who called for help is Janis Joplin. She and her boyfriend were involved in some love stunt that put her car in a ditch. When she opens her wallet to pay me all I see are fifties and hundreds."

This is either primo bullshit or God's honest truth. It doesn't matter at McMurdo – the clock won't tick any quicker. I'm sounding more redneck every day. My New York accent is a melting. I wish I had the balls to speak up and return serve to Mumma. How do you follow a tale that drops the name of a rock star?

I come up with the name Kelley's Heroes for the firehouse basketball team because Frank chucks in half our baskets and Don Rickles starred in the movie. He played a ball-breaking little guy. When we see Edward G. Robinson in a flick as the fast-talking gangster Rico, I get tagged with the name. I've been called worse.

Kees and I play guard, Ed and Frank are forwards and Andy is our center because he can't dribble and won't try to learn. McCracken was our center but he ate so slow he missed practice. He went to the COMMSARPS team with Fang and Marty. We lost a sensitive center. Not every game is competitive but the few Seabees here will put an elbow to my chin or a knee to my nuts. I carry the badge of dishonor for having punched a Seabee in the face. It's not a big deal-the real assholes went home with the summer crew.

When the game begins, Chief Condon referees and the first minutes are played with an ice cold basketball. No fouls are called until the Chief warms his whistle. Frank and Ed throw jumpers from the top of the key that put the game out of reach by half-time. I like to dribble in and feed Andy who refuses to move from under the basket. We start calling him Paint Man. I don't want to sound modest but I scored 10 points.

5/2. SSS -Interview with Meher Baba

I climb Observation Hill to seek out our local Holy Man, Mr. Meher Baba. I find him sitting with his feet in his lap and his arms across his chest. His exploding hair and beard are Pytlik's wet dream.

SSS: Mr. Baba can I call you Meher?

Baba:

SSS: Do you carry any kind of ID?

Baba:

SSS: I wouldn't want to be interviewing the wrong holy man.

Baba:

SSS: What's it like living up here on this frozen mountain top?

Baba:

SSS: Let me guess – you're doing that no talking routine.

Baba:

I conclude the interview in order to make my deadline.

5/2. We stay in touch with our loved ones via phone patch and MARSGRAM. A MARSGRAM is a hard copy radio transmission that reaches you through our Comshack.

MARSGRAM 2 MAY 1971

HI LOVER, YOU ARE TRYING TO DRIVE ME INSANE.
EITHER THAT OR KEEP ME BUSY TRYING TO FIGURE
OUT MYSTERIOUS PUZZLES. I HAVE TRIED EVERY
WAY TO FIGURE IT OUT. I STILL CAN'T GUESS WHY I
AM FAMOUS.I HAVE THE TWO ALBUMS – AERIAL
BALLET AND NIELSEN SINGS NEWMAN. THEY ARE
BOTH GREAT. I JUST GOT MELANIE'S LATEST ALBUM -
THE GOOD BOOK-IT'S FANTASTIC. MY SONG TO YOU
IS 'I'LL BE HOME'. I AM AND WILL BE WAITING FOR
YOU IN OCTOBER –'YOU CAN COUNT ON ME"
BECAUSE I LOVE YOU. YOUR KATHY

5/5. Frank and I are on fire patrol. We're inspecting
Quonset huts abandoned for the winter. Looking for
anything not secured, we break into the bottom
drawer of a locked desk. There we uncover the erotic
equivalent of the Dead Sea scrolls. A glossy full-color
catalogue of German porno that requires no
translation includes a photo of a girl and an excited
horse. Beneath that a stack of cheaper skin rags, the

type that sit on the shelf above Playboy. Frank drops them as if they're radioactive. All the models are black. He decides I keep these. He takes the one with Sea Biscuit's chick. I don't object. All naked women are my type.

5/7. We call Lt. Goepfert "Goofy Grape" but not to his face. He comes to the firehouse to do a zone inspection. We are carrying on the Navy traditions that embody cleanliness and order. After he passes us, Ed and I go to special services and draw out boxing gloves and a heavy bag.

5/8. We play volleyball and win two out of three. At 2200, Andy, Hobson and I take on Suicide Hill in banana sleds. I ride all the way down to a wipeout that feels like a car crash. I stumble back to my rack. Behind my bird cloth curtain I review my Nubian harem.

5/10 Eddie and I spar in the garage. Eddy is fast and hard to pin against a fire truck. Chief Condon spars with Arfy.

5/10 MARSGRAM

PETE

BIG NEWS- BARBARA HAD A SEVEN POUND NINE OUNCE GIRL ON FRIDAY. KATHY HILL AND I WENT SATURDAY TO VISIT THEM AT THE HOSPITAL. NEEDLESS TO SAY THE PROUD PARENTS WERE BEAMING. BABYS NAME IS PATRICIA ANN. SAD NEWS IS I LOST THE STONE IN YOUR NAVY RING. I WAS QUITE UPSET. I LOST IT AT A SHOWER I WENT TO IN THE BRONX LAST SUNDAY. BUT I STILL WEAR IT. IT WAS ONLY THE STONE –AS LONG AS I DON'T EVER LOSE YOU I'LL EXIST.

YOUR KATHY

5/11. Homer approves of my suggestion that we paint the inside of the firehouse. Faced with nothing else to do, Frank, Eddie and I can stretch this job out for a month or more. We propose an early start, early lunch, daily nooners and an early field day. Kees, Arfy, Laine and Andy can devise their own plans to stay busy. Homer likes the idea because we'll be in the house and he will be free to roam around town lobbying officers in his crusade to make Chief.

5/13. Mac, Roger and I get high in the laundry.

5/15. When I was a kid and knew I was going to the dentist I would start crying in the car.

"Why are you crying, he hasn't hurt you yet?" My father would ask.

Once I was big enough to escape a grown man, I never returned for a checkup. At boot camp twenty four cavities of mine were repaired by guys my own age. When Doc Esquire looks into my mouth his brow collapses.

"You're in a world of shit."

I'm now on his calendar twice a week. He issues me dental floss.

5/16. A week after our paint party is approved we start to put paint on the wall. Around a roller pan, we're the Three Stooges. Frank has taped off all the molding that arcs up and across our ceiling. Using extensions we roll white as high as we can reach. Navy blue on the lower wall will give the effect of wainscoting. With no painter's caps, we wear underpants on our heads.

5/16.   SSS- From the Diary of Doctor Dish

In present company, I run a gauntlet of puns designed to unnerve me. I've yet to behead anyone for their cornball turn on my name but the day is not over. I will not be returning to the world I came from. My only ambition is to act on a grand scale.

My name is Dish, Carl Dish. I know – you thought I ran away with the spoon. I'm a scientist working alongside sailors who think they're funny. Talking only to myself, I declare Antarctic citizenship. Others may visit but I'm relocating. My waking hours are spent among Navy support staff. On May 8, 1965, I intend to bid them a silent adieu. In the meantime they can cook, do my laundry and take turns at comedy.

"Dish, do you bowl?"

"Are you from China?

"Smells like fish, not for Dish." This navy bromide haunts me because of an opinion I should have kept to myself. As a microbiologist I'm aware of the level of bacteria present in the vagina and I warned my mates of the danger of spreading infection via oral sex. It has inspired stabs from the crew.

"Carl won't feast, if he sees yeast.

"Two things that won't go down – the sun and Doctor Dish.

Disappearing from Longwire is more appealing every time I consider it. How would I hide in the widest open space in the world? I can see myself confounding this simple team. When I'm wearing my white hair net and lab coat I already resemble a snowman.

I have put myself in charge of my own kidnapping. I plan to follow the wind along a crested whitecap dividing madness from imagination. I've tested the route on field trips. The wind will erase my footprints.

Shackleton, Byrd and Perry all went north at the end of the day. I, Carl Robert Dish renounce my American citizenship. I'm asking the ice for asylum. I will be a one man government serving a one man population. Essential to my escape is to leave without leaving tracks.

5/17. Frank, Ed and I go to the galley and cook our own eggs. We're spending the morning touching up the white paint we've rolled on yesterday and cutting in with blue on the lower part of the wall. After our nooners we clean our brushes and go to lift weights.

5/23   SSS-Interview with Frank "Fang" Lucas

Fang should be rocking in a body bag by the time you read this. He will be remembered as a good natured radioman, an exacting assistant editor and a half-ass sailor. Unfortunate for Frank, he chose to make fun of Cynthia Meyers. Perhaps his bitterness at being not short enough led to drinking, gambling and inconsiderate remarks. One of Cynthia's many admirers slipped a poison in his tea. Our interview begins right after he is informed he has thirty minutes to live.

Frank was born in Yreka California- population 5,000. His Dad and Granddad ran Swallows Auto Court. (Insert swallow joke here). While in high school he worked as a dishwasher at the El Rancho Café. Frank was temporary Class Vice President when the incumbent was impeached for cutting classes.

March of 1968 a breeze across his neck inspired Frank to "Go Navy". Boot camp was San Diego, followed by basic electronics followed by 14 weeks of radioman "A" school. Before deploying to Guam his house burned down. He picked up 15 days of emergency leave and his soon to be widowed wife Candy.

While waiting for his life to slip away he answered the following inquiries.

SSS: Frank, you burned your house down to get extra leave?

Frank: Is that a question?

SSS: Considering you're playing out the last minutes of your existence, what are your thoughts and feelings?

Frank: What's the movie tonight?

SSS: You're not going to be around to see it. Why did you have to be so critical of a guy's girlfriend – you know-the guy who poisoned you.

Frank: I didn't mean to defile his sacred cow.

SSS: See what I mean? If you could spend these last few minutes alive convincing someone of something – who and what would it be?

Frank: I'd try to get Nixon to pull his head out of his ass. What the fuck do we care if Mao has another twenty million mouths to feed? Let the whole world go commie-I'll fight when they hit the Pacific Highway.

SSS: How you feeling?

Frank: Is it warm in here?

SSS: Do you want to make any kind of apology while you can?

Frank: Cynthia dear, I'm sorry I uddered a word about you. You can't be blamed for the low IQ of your fan base.

SSS: Die you bastard.

Editors Note: Frank got the runs and nothing else. He continues his work at SSS and as town roustabout. Wish him well while you have the chance

5/26. Mac, Roger Turner and I get high in the laundry.

5/28. I find tape on Jimi Hendrix's face and my poster of Fu Man Chu. Tape Man is elusive as the Viet Cong.

5/29.   My teeth are bothering me now that they've been fixed. I take four aspirins after lunch and sleep till 1600. After evening chow I spar two rounds with Fast Eddie and one with McCracken. The movie is Shock Troops. I brush my teeth before bed – something I haven't been doing. Dr. Esquire has me in the cult of dental floss.

5/30.   SSS Interview with Russ Peterman

With no access to sports broadcasts we turn our attention to science. Our mission here is to support scientific research. We are assigned to a nerd continent. The nerdiest among us is Russ Peterman from satellite tracking. In the mess hall Russ explains the irreversibility of mixing gases –it's Mexican night. Russ wears his hair long and walks around in street clothes. He gets paid a civilian salary.

SSS: Russ, are we supposed to kiss your ass because you graduated college?

Russ: Actually, I am finishing my last year of college while I'm down here.

SSS You're getting civilian pay while down here, finishing college and enjoying a draft deferment. How did you pull that off?

Russ: I'm a scientist.

SSS: Like the Russian dude who tried to make friends with The Thing?

Russ: Pretty much me without the beaver hat.

SSS: Do we need to fear you?

Russ: Let's see how the interview goes.

SSS: Tell our readers about yourself, please.

Russ: I was born in Fredericksburg, Texas. My Dad was a carpenter – just like Jesus. We moved to Austin where I was third string quarterback for Lanier High. I scrambled more than a short order chef then let the ball fly, often completing passes to people standing on the sidelines.

SSS: Did you know Kees played on a championship team from Sweeney, Texas?

Russ: The Bulldogs, I remember because he's told me a hundred times.

SSS: Russ, you got married before coming to the ice.

Russ: Is that a question?

SSS: How was your honeymoon?

Russ: Traditional. Tommye stayed with me all the way to ChiChi.

SSS: You married a girl named Tommye?

Russ: Is that a question?

SSS: You're pretty much a ball-breaker. In two words how can we improve life at McMurdo?

Russ: Less Navy.

SSS: Ouch. Your job here is to track satellites. All of them are ours?

Russ: You have a funny way of asking questions.

SSS: Fess up Russ, are you doing side work for the Russians?

Russ: I am not a spy.

SSS: There's a rumor you banged the blonde off the Lindblad.

Russ: That would be the rumor you just made up.

SSS: What about UFO's have you seen any?

Russ: You know my work is classified.

SSS: I'll take that as a "Yes". Okay pocket protector – would you, if ordered, shoot down a Russian satellite?

Russ: Depends on what's smoking at the firehouse.

SSS: No further questions.

Russ: Promise?

Russ turns a salt shaker in a clockwise orbit while turning himself counter-clockwise. He's demonstrating some satellite phenomena to Tress who is eating chili. His remark about the firehouse has ended the interview. Talk like that will only support a popular suspicion.

5/31. Frank, Eddie and I have an informal agreement that we not wake each other up. It's hard to get to sleep and once you go out you might as well capitalize on it. We are to snap awake at the sound of the fire alarm; otherwise we self-reveille. After lunch I get up late from my nap. Frank is painting and Eddie is asleep. Around 1600 Eddie joins me hitting the heavy bag. After evening chow we watch PM3A play the Dispensables in low scoring basketball. Pretty Poison is the movie. We lift weights before Mid-rats. Big eye keeps us no-sleepwalking.

 I try to interview guys who don't eat at the same table as me. Guys usually sit with the other guys from their shop class- just like high school. I target -Chief Dinsmore and Charlie Webb. I'll even interview a Seabee.

The Chaplin contributes a written sermon to every issue of our paper. The old man writes a Captain's Corner. There's a funny question and answer column by a guy named Gabby. Hand drawn cartoons, a personals page and local sports scores are bound by a corner staple. Each edition is 90 copies; readers are expected to pass them around.

6/1. Homer wakes me for my phone patch at 1730. Kathy is so sweet. She says, "It's a really different Memorial Day." Last year, we spent this weekend alone together.

6/2. We are scheduled to attend an award ceremony this morning but arrive late. The Old Man sends us back to the firehouse. Homer is pissed at Kees. At night we play the Dispensables a close game. The movie is For A Few Bullets More. We're adrift in a sea of slack. It's starting to sink in – we're painting too fast.

6/5. I score 18 points in our victory over Public Works.

6/6. We are putting a second coat of white on the truck bay. Spending as much time cleaning our brushes and rollers as we are adding paint to the wall, we struggle to keep this job unfinished.

6/7 Mac's birthday -we drink beer and eat cheese sandwiches.

6/8. We move on to painting the inside of firehouse doors. At the dentist I get two more defective fillings replaced. Our paint job looks good as we've gone over it a dozen times. Tonight's movie is <u>Victory At Sea</u>.

6/10. Fast Eddie goes across the street to mess cook. Frank and I expand the paint job to include every wall on the firehouse ground floor. At 2100 we lift weights till 2230 then I hit the heavy bag which is now hanging in the laundry. After a shower, I'm in my rack and unable to sleep.

6/11. Andy is at ringside watching Ed and I spar. It goes without saying he's waiting his turn. There's competitiveness between us, I'm willing to indulge. I know he walks around thinking he could kick my ass if he really had to. For a guy who's done so many mind expanding drugs he has some school yard attitudes. Andy would thrive in Vietnam.

When he gets in the ring he squares up in this funny kangaroo stance. After I land a three punch combination, I drop my face into his rising right hand. He's knocked my front teeth out. We can't look at each other without smirking. Fang laughs when he sees me at chow.

What Andy knocked out were two false teeth held in by spit and grade school paste. They were mismatched replacements installed when the originals were knocked out in high school horseplay. Andy has done me a favor. Just when I thought I was finishing up with the dentist I'm back in his chair. I call LCDR Robert Esquire "Doc". At 5"5' he gets the Snow White reference.

"Not the first time I heard that."

His assistant, Fred Nevill is 6'2" to make matters worse. When Fred farts the two of them run outside. I'm left in the chair like a man on death row.

Doc started out as a sculptor until he saw the wage gap. Being a dentist makes him an officer who doesn't act like an officer. He acts like a dentist and a lobbyist for dental floss.

6/15. When we played the Dispensables the other night, Doc dribbled up to me, I stole the ball and reversed field. Ahead of the pack I made an easy layup. Today I'm in his chair with my yap wide open.

"You know you embarrassed me?" He's waving a drill that hasn't been turned on. I hope he's making a joke. I'm a crybaby when it comes to pain. There's no effective apology with a mouth full of cotton.

6/16. Roger Turner advises me that our Carl Dish saga is considered offensive. I'm supposed to talk to the Old Man.

6/19. The movie is <u>The Vengeance of Fu Manchu</u>.
We're sparring in the laundry now because it's too
cold to do it anywhere else. I go two rounds with Ed
and two with a Kiwi who comes to town just for this.
I've boxed as a teenager in a Police Club so I have a
grip on this sport. These other guys would love to
land a clean punch. I can't afford to let them. I've just
had my front teeth replaced.

6/20. SSS-Interview with HMC Bob Dinsmore

Bob Dinsmore was holding four sevens when his
poker game was interrupted by 81 mortars raining
down on Marble Mountain, Da Nang. Drawing
shrapnel in his hip and a cut on the neck he was
hospitalized overnight but resumed duty as the
Patient Affairs Officer the following morning. Later in
that tour he was one of the stretcher crew who
brought the escaped American POW Denzler into
camp. "The NVA knew we had him so we got hit hard
that night."

We meet with the Chief in his room where he sips hard liquor.

SSS: Chief four sevens or 81 mortars – which is harder to believe?

Chief: Are you expecting me to take a polygraph?

SSS: Tell our readers a little about your career?

Chief: I've been in for eighteen years and I'm 35 years old. I've never been at any command long enough to like it. I'll retire with 19 years, 7 months and 24 days – does it sound like I'm counting?

SSS: Did you ever wish you weren't a dick-checker?

Chief: If I wasn't a Corpsman I wouldn't have stayed in the navy.

SSS: What has the Navy done for you?

Chief: I finished high school, got some college credits. Traveled to Gitmo, Okinawa, Nam and the ice plus a dozen other stateside assignments.

SSS: You've worked with the Marines quite a bit. Tell our readers about that.

Chief: I worked the brig at Camp LeJuene then transferred to Marine Recruit Depot at Parris Island. A Staff Sgt McKenna marched his people into a swamp and six men drowned. I remember Walther Winchell saying." If you have a son in Korea, write to him, if you have a son at Parris Island, pray for him." I drove the ambulance to pick up the dead.

SSS: Yikes, tell us about Okinawa.

Chief: I was attached to fleet marines at Camp Butler. When my four year old son was hit by a car and was in critical condition, I was sent home and assigned to the Naval Reserve Center in Hazelton Pa. When my son recovered they sent me to Nam.

SSS: What do you think of the current changes in the Navy?

Chief: I don't like the change in uniform. It's one thing to be an officer or make the hat. If you're an E6 or lower you want to look like a sailor.

SSS: What was the most interesting patient you ever worked on – you don't have to say me.

Chief: I was serving with my uncle in Nam. He was a Captain in the Medical Corp. He was called to work on a Vietnamese civilian. Along with a First Class EDD they successfully removed a mortar from the guy's chest. I set up the sandbags around the OR. My uncle got the Navy Cross and the EDD was meritoriously advanced to Chief.

SSS: You didn't mention my time in sick bay.

Chief: I wish we could have pulled your head out of your ass.

SSS: Ouch. Chief cuts reporter and then sews him up. What is the first thing you want to do when you get off the ice?

Chief: Get laid. Yeah put that in.

SSS: Have you ever been on the other side of the stethoscope?

Chief: Onboard the U.SS. Horne DLG 30 I pulled a hernia that put me in the San Diego hospital for 44 days. I can't say a bad word about how I was treated.

 SSS: To what extent do you think drugs are a problem in the navy?

Chief: It's not the biggest problem but we have to get rid of those who corrupt their shipmates.

SSS: You looked at me when you said that.

Chief: Thanks for the interview.

6/22. The base shuts down for our Mid-Winter Party. It takes place in the mess hall where a banner announces it as The Big Eyeball. There is a stage for people to get up and pose on. If you brought any civilian clothes with you, today is the day to break them out. A Seabee, CS2 Law comes to the party in a harem two piece with a veil to cover his beard. His hairless arms and legs seem womanly. Everyone is drunk or in a hurry to get there.

"Who's taking you home?" I hear Law asked, more than once.

Someone is coveting thy neighbor's ass. Homer is dressed as a fatter than most fire hydrant. Bill Baker wears a gas mask to top off a swamp thing costume. Roger Turner and Tim Groshong are in drag and it doesn't appear to be their first time at sea. Everyone is smoking and drinking, officers are serving as busboys. There's music blasting and we're having wine with filet mignon. The Kiwis start singing and we run back to the firehouse. Stick, Andy, Ed, John, Dave, Fang, Howie and McGranaghan all share a few bowls. Then some of us take mescaline. Back at the mess hall no one has missed us. Fast Eddie takes the stage and starts a routine no one can hear.

Wearing his white busboy cap and field greens he pumps his arms to emphasize points to the blurred congregation. Ice cream is served with chocolate syrup. On Main Street we drag each other around on a banana sled. The winter is counting down by the time we hit our racks.

6/26. I always seem to be the last man up. Ed, Frank and I were supposed to do a skit at the Midwinter Party but when the time came I balked. I could blame it on being high. Often you have so much going on inside your head; you avoid anything more complicated than sitting still. They are ranking on me because I was the one daring them to do it and even conducted a rehearsal. Drugs do affect your performance, I know Dad.

6/28. Haddock drives me to flammable stores to draw down black and yellow paint. Back at the firehouse I'm told I should have got grey as well. We do field day, lunch and then return to get the grey. The paint must warm up before we use it. Working in close quarters we deliberately bump each other, hide things and make art of breaking chops.

6/30. The tradition of securing at mid-day on Wednesdays is called rope yarn. Ask a lifer because I don't know why. Frank and I are at the movie exchange when Chaplain Lesher walks in. Frank drops to the floor and starts sobbing,

"Forgive me Father, I've jerked off."

Back at the firehouse, I get word I can phone patch Kathy. Playing cards, I lose the six dollars I drew at pay this morning.

Reviewing my diary, I'm shocked at my amount of rack time. Most days it's no less than 10 hours of vertical but I'm not always asleep. I battle with big eye. I've scented my pillow, hung a black curtain and used a length of line to tie myself to my rack. Nothing guarantees sleep. Beer makes me sleepy but then I have to get up to go below and use the head. Our baker, Roger Turner, suggests I take a pod of unbaked dough to bed with me. It's too creepy to be considered.

7/1. There is a fire in Hut 52. I jump into truck 3, my assigned Nodwell. While the other trucks race out of the house I get boxed into a corner beside the open doors. I'm inching forward and back like a fat man in quick sand. Every switch of gears stalls the truck. When I arrive at the fire a half hour late, I get a round of applause from my mates.

7/2. My Pace course final in philosophy allows me eight hours to complete two questions. It's our worst weather yet -45F and that's not wind chill. I take the test back to my rack – hoping philosophy will make me sleepy.

I expound on the question of an all-knowing God vs. man's free will. I propose that once God is conceived he refuses to be unconceived. That man volunteers to abandon his fear of free will by putting God in charge of whatever happens. It's an enlistment we make that frees us from answering for our part in war.

7/3. No amount of touching up can justify the continued painting of the firehouse. Homer orders us to strip the paint off our trucks and repaint them. I'm assigned to Nodwell 3 and I paint a block shaped 3 on the door that no one likes.

7/4. The Fourth of July carnival kicks off and involves a base wide day off. No one represents the firehouse at the chow hall fair. We're a clique of girl scouts quick to change our mood. We're having our own party in the firehouse and people are stopping by. John shows up with prizes he won throwing darts. Homer is drinking. He says "nigger" in front of Phil Toussaint and we all shake our heads. He'll never make Chief with his mouth. You don't piss off the cook, even I know that.

At the mess there is a pie eating contest, arts and crafts and Mr. Flick blowing glass (insert blowing joke). I go over with John and bring back soup. Our movie is <u>Wait Until Dark</u>.

7/7. Homer's in a mood. It's -40F in the truck bay and he expects us to paint. I bring the laundry across the street to Mac and rap to him. He's half on the rag most of the time. When we get around to painting it's the passageway beside the 2nd class quarters. We break at 1130, nap till 1430 and then lift weights. At 2300 we go to mid-rats. I'm eating more than I ever ate as a civilian.

Lifting weights is a bore. Frank and I force each other to go to the improvised weight room. Once in awhile, other guys are there when we arrive. Doing bench presses in a room where it's too cold to sweat and too small to stretch results in little result. I'm eating so much I'm certain I'll get fat if I don't stay active. I tape a photo of Dick Gregory inside Frank's hat. I put toothpaste on his girlfriend's picture and tape on his LSU logo.

7/9 Doctor McDonald is our inspecting officer. Laine is charged with escorting him around. We're committed to scheduled inspections just as strict as any command ship. Frank and I have conducted field day. Eddie is across the street playing mess cook. Homer calls me in his room to have me repeat my objections to taking the latest advancement exam.

7/10. I help Neeley write an article for our paper about the proper protocol for making a phone patch. Guys forget that there are two ham radio operators listening in on every exchange. Others will complain about the poor connection rather than concentrate on what they can hear. Badmouthing other men at base is stupid. Why would your family at home want to hear that?

7/11. The firehouse movie room is standing room only for <u>Bonnie and Clyde</u>. Faye Dunaway slips into my rack beside me. I'm rethinking the idea of the baker's dough.

7/12. Orders are arriving. Homer gets a reserve DD the U.S.S. Hank out of Philadelphia. He'll be able to go home on a three day weekend. Homer gets drunk to celebrate. Some Seabees are going back to Nam.

7/13. Andy bowls a 213. Things come easy to this kid. He's the type of guy you would find hanging around a bowling alley but never paying for a game. We're the best of friends except when we're not. I don't blame him for knocking out my teeth. I have a better looking front grill than I had before. With a mouthpiece, I would have kicked his ass.

"You didn't knock me out, you knocked my teeth out," I remind him.

7/15. I draw $74 in pay. I give Frank $4, Homer $2 and Laine $1. These are my short pots in poker. We spend the morning taking the trucks out of the house and then putting them back in. Someone says its -120F by wind chill, the coldest day of our tour. Fang, Mike, Mac and I smoke until Frank comes to get me to go lift weights. Frank is in a great mood. His orders are for shore duty in Charleston.

7/16. Lunch is shrimp, lobster, lasagna and pie. I'm eating everything that comes near me. In the afternoon I paint my truck while Frank goes to sign his orders. I have to paint over the improvised 3 on the side of my truck. Navy issued stencils are the only authorized insignia. I hate erasing it, I thought I drew a really cool 3. After evening chow Frank and I sit with Ken Farley for his SSS interview. He's one of the most low-key guys on the base. I start the interview by asking if he's a secret agent.

7/17. At a nuclear plant decontamination drill, the firehouse crew single files toward the exit. We make-believe take off Haz-Mat suits then step into an open stall to take a make-believe shower. I'm behind Fast Eddie. When he steps into the stall he looks back at me, sticks his tongue out and pulls the shower curtain closed. I find this is snot blowing funny.

LCDR Arcuni, our Engineering Officer, asks Homer to poll his crew on what the fuck is so funny about decontamination. He expects a written response. Homer is pissed at me but I blame Eddie's. He's so funny I can't even look at him.

7/19. Immersed in Meher Baba's writings, I elect to fast. I want to see if a few days without food will enlighten me, spiritually. Twenty eight hours after I start keeping track, I'm tearing into a can of melon balls with the batwing can-opener from the firehouse kitchen. It's a Beat the Clock skit, with me shoveling melon balls in my mouth to stave off fainting. I feel Jesus smack me across the back of the head. I'm dizzy and weak. It's essential to eat and sleep well at this base. I'm expected to fight a fire if we ever get a real one. It's my duty to be fit for duty.

Give a kid a basketball and a playground and leave him alone all day – he'll get better at basketball. Getting high so often should make me better at being high but each step off the curb is its own school crossing. You can't rely on past experiences. Each dive from the high board holds the potential for a belly flop. I shiver when I recall the poison.

Many insights occur under party lights. It dawns on me that everything I think I know I don't know and that people see me walking around with masking tape stuck on my back.

At the radio station I come in an hour before my show to observe the other DJ's. Tim Hobson calls himself the "Mad Tooth", Rich Wilson is now "The Savior" and Dale Thomas calls himself "The Grape." Fang is Fang. I haven't picked an on air name because they all sound so stupid. I'm not using "The Voice of New York." If I wanted to make fun of other guy's accents, I'd be busy all day. Firehouse Pete is lame and I'm resisting Rico but you have to have a name if you're doing radio.

Behind the control board, I bond with overnight DJ's from around the globe. I'm broadcasting to God knows who. McMurdo is a gold mine of insomnia so chances are I have at least one listener. I try to make art by playing records. The menu provides an insight into my sensitivities. If I'm high, the show improves from my perspective.

7/19. Homer and Frank attack me while I'm lying on my rack. My mattress follows us to the floor where we wrestle until everything around us has tipped over. I'm left with the mess to clean up. Homer and Frank go to the club to continue drinking.

Gambling plays a part in passing time. You can win money by betting people they can't name the day of the week. Shifts and hours are intertwined as clothes in a tumble dry. I bet Nealey he can't name the date and the month.

"Why do you care, what day it is, Boot? You're not going home ahead of me. When you don't see me you're getting short."

7/22. The outbreak of crime continues. Someone taped McCracken's doughnut to a shelf in the laundry. Nine candy bars are missing from Homer's nightstand. Nine watches are still missing from the ships store. We consider a police blotter for the Sunday paper.

7/28. Breaking my rule never to go anywhere with Arfy, we take an uneventful ride to Scott Base. In Scott's cabin, half eaten meals on chipped plates ring the dining table. It appears the crew has been called outside and never returned. Conrad's an alright guy, I forgive everything but the hairbrush. After chow tonight, I get a phone patch home. Mom tells me my brother Tom is getting married.

I pretend I have a secret identity that no one who knows me knows. Smooth as a jewel thief, I shift to a spirit world, as difficult to define as "pernicious." I wield super powers of counter-intelligence. I'm a pro at propaganda and subterfuge but I am not the watch thief.

7/29. Mr. Goepfert and Chief Lakey search our quarters. Pytlik is sure the watches were taken this week as he had just updated his inventory. There's no outgoing flight so they have to be somewhere in this world. During my radio show I conduct a mock telephone call with the man holding the watches for ransom.

"Nine watches for nine candy bars." I pretend to bargain an exchange of Timex for chocolates. I'm representing the culprit in the Homer break-in. No one thinks it's funny or admits it is. On Rich Wilson's show he tears into the thief with words that border on beepable.

"You are scum, an embarrassment to this command, an idiot, a loser, a disgrace to the Navy. I hope you have the little bit of balls it will take to return the watches. No questions asked except the ones you ought to be asking yourself."

7/30. The Waggoner is a sled that carries five hundred gallons of water in a red tank. Left outside to freeze last season, it sits at the bottom of a list of equipment to be rescued. I sit atop the tank and chip ice from a man-hole sized opening with a hammer and chisel. After lunch Homer brings an acetylene torch and we take turns melting ice an easier way. The fumes from the torch can't be avoided. We get gas in our lungs. Chief Condon orders me to sick bay. After chow we play Crazy 8's.

8/1. Sunday, I attend the cruise book meeting. We discuss proposed titles. I suggest Ordeal in Darkness and the table cracks up because they see I'm serious. After that remark anything I say is dismissed or not commented on at all. The cruise book title is A Winter's Reflection. Tonight's movie is Sgt. Ryker.

8/3. Reading my diary the same words repeat - rack, mid-rats, big eye, read, write, movie, nooners and skate. We are in the tar pit of this tour. Counting days only slows them down but I count anyway. Sometimes I can't muster the energy to play cards.

8/4. Commander Maddox comes to the firehouse to present Frank with the Sailor of the Month award. We clap hands and take pictures. John completes his third year of Navy today so we take the hash pipe to the radio station and celebrate. I don't think in terms of discharge. I might be short for McMurdo but I owe Uncle Sam two years after I get off the ice.

8/7. John and I take half hits of mescaline and play cards in his room. A Seabee named Hair has his tape recorder playing Gordon Lightfoot non- stop. You can hear it from down the hall.

8/8. I'm not sleeping for three days now. The mescaline works as speed and I wasn't sleepy when I took it. I lie in my rack reading or writing in my diary. Between bowling, ping pong, pool and the movies there's hardly anything to do. I could lift weights, spar or play cards. I apologize to myself about the mood I'm in.

8/12. My orders arrive; I'm assigned to the U.S. S. Simon Lake ASG 33out of Charleston, South Carolina, same base Frank is going to. I'm on a ship after two years in the Navy. I wonder if they have pussy in Charleston.

8/14. Frank goes to the galley to serve his time. I type up my interview with Tom Roy. At the message center I phone patch Kathy and tell her about my orders. I mention us going to Charleston together. My cruise box is built with Arfy's carpenters' precision. I'm going to paint it up and watch the clock with everyone else. We have under a month of winter.

I meet with the Old Man. He explains his concern about Doctor Dish's family one day asking him why he allowed this to go on.

"I'm not censuring anyone but I want you to think about how that man's Mother would feel knowing you made fun of him and I let you."

At the fire house, I find out it's too late to pull my recent Carl Dish story, the issue has gone to press.

8/15. SSS-From the Diary of Doctor Dish

"Carl, I'm wet." In the gagging heat of the summerhouse her voice made everything warmer. The blonde hair over one eye threw shade on her cheerleader smile. Her fingers rolled down her pink panties, marked with a dark spot centered as a dot on a map. Passing over one knee and then another they flew into the corner of the room.

"Am I scaring you, Carl?" She ran her hand between her legs.

"Gee ma nee!" My throat was filled with sand. Crossing her arms she peeled off her tank top and two pink breasts popped out like kittens sniffing a new morning.

"These are your toys, Carl."

She brushed her hands across them to insure no misunderstanding. She was offering herself to me. My shorts got tight and sweat rolled down my back. I wanted to open a window but was afraid to move.

"Make me do things, Carl. The other girls say you're shy but I think you're pretending." Taking a step backwards she dropped onto the couch, legs apart as a clothespin. "All that kissing made me tinkle." The hand between her legs was making a sound. A pink fingernail disappeared inside her.

"Carl are you going to put a baby inside me?"

My hand touched a cold wall and I sat upright as if surprised by a movie's sudden ending. Alone, assumed dead and thousands of miles away from a summerhouse, I am Carl Dish, a scientist with a wet dream. Fifteen months since I've seen another human and ten weeks since I ate my dog. I am free of everything except lust in my sleep. I answer to no woman. Only in my unconscious am I a slave. Awake I own my appetites.

In this back porch of the world Mother Nature wears a shawl. The Antarctic gets no hurricanes, tornadoes, mud slides, forest fires or tsunamis. I'm safer here than a lot of other places. This place has never been invaded, sacked by Mongols or leveled by plague. What I don't have is indoors. Other than my solar condom sleeping chamber I'm outside the walls of what surrounds everyone else. Don't pity me, I'm busy pitying you.

8/15.   SSS Interview with Tom Roy.

Tom Roy out of Marquette, Michigan, ran the mile in high school. As a paperboy he delivered the Mining Journal for $45 a week. After two years of business administration at Northern Michigan University Tom's draft card was burning a hole in his pocket.

He was buttonholed by a navy recruiter after having enlisted in the army. He turned Tom around and watched him rip up his army contract.

After San Diego boot camp Tom piped aboard the U.S.S. Sperry AS12 berthed three blocks away from his recruit training. He took liberty in Tijuana where he drank and watched naked women dance. He also took weekends in Palm Springs (insert palm joke).

Tom moved on to the U.S.S. Greenlite and rode her from Subic Bay to San Diego for her decommissioning. Next stop Davisville and then the ice on October 10. Our interview took place at mid-rats where Tom's co-worker Vernon Buck kicked him in the leg every time he said "Probably."

SSS: Is this the most depressing time of your life?

Tom: Probably when I was around thirteen, I thought everyone was picking on me. That was a bad time for me. Down here I know who's picking on me and I don't give a crap.

SSS: Any suggestions on improving things on base?

Tom: Heat the Admin building, soundproof 155 and why the hell can't we grow fresh vegetables?

SSS: As opposed to canned?

Tom: Don't pick on me.

SSS: You're in personnel. Do you find most people unhappy with the way the Navy handles their personnel affairs?

Tom: Probably more unhappy than they need to be. Look, I handle a lot of files – you handle your own (insert handle joke). If you're expecting me to remind you that you're up for an award or accrued leave you're gonna be disappointed. We have short people stocking high shelves so don't expect those around you to be any more competent than you are.

SSS: What motto do you live by?

Tom: Do unto others before they do onto you.

SSS: What do you consider success?

Tom: Probably money enough to cover bail. Good friends, good music, heat – heat is probably the most important part of success at this time in my life. Ouch.

SSS: Any disappointments with this tour?

Tom: I expected to be living in a Jamesway with storms banging on the windows and blizzards sweeping under the door. The winter here is milder than at home.

SSS: Who would you like to see visit McMurdo?

Tom: Richard Nixon, I would like to lock him in the EM club until he stopped the war.

SSS: Easy Tommy, let's not get too radical.

Tom: Probably people calling me Tommy is one of my biggest complaints.

SSS: Sorry, name a movie that describes this command.

Tom: Ship of Fools.

SSS: A cause you would demonstrate or picket for"

Tom: Probably the environment.

SSS: If you could bring anything home from McMurdo what would it be?

Tom: Nine watches.

8/17. Today seems like yesterday over again. Chores around the house are broken up by four meals at the galley. At night I smoke hash with the stoner squad then we play ping pong into the middle of the third shift. Homer finds me awake at reveille. I'm reading One Flew Over the Cuckoo's Nest.

8/18. More than one lifer has suggested that the Carl Dish articles are disrespectful. At the message center I'm put on trial. I contend that by providing a motive for his disappearance I have elevated the act. That doesn't justify this past week's wet dream entry. A USARP named Fritz sees me in the mess hall and rubs his hands together.

"More scintillating thigh stories.'

8/19. No explanation for the mood I'm in. I plop in Homer's easy chair and dream awake about places covered in earlier diaries. I'm hitchhiking at night in upstate New York; I hear dogs barking in far off yards.

My brother Tom and I are on a high school bus trip to the Washington D.C.. We both wish we were doing something else. Halfway home from the beach I realize I left the pinkie ring Kathy gave me, lying somewhere in the sand. We turn around and go back and after a five minute search of the area we think we were sitting in, she finds it.

8/20. I'm huddled around the pipe with John, Mike and Fang. Homer knocks and enters; something he never does.

"Kearney, the Chaplain needs to see you in my room." Homer says. The sewing circle whoops until Homer makes a face.

"Carl Dish is going to the gallows," Mike suggests as I get up. I can't believe it. Has the Old Man sent the Chaplain here to chew my ass over that stupid story? Chaplain Lesher, standing in Homer's room, tells me my brother has been killed.

"Which brother?"

"Arthur, in a helicopter crash in Germany."

"You're sure."

"You will phone patch with your Dad in the morning."

"Yes sir."

Back in my room I break the news to the crew. I lie down on my rack and they go to mid-rats. There's nothing anyone can say to make things other than what they are.

8/21. I phone patch Dad and he breaks the news all over again.

"It's bad. You're Mother and sisters are in a fury. I wish you were here."

"I wish I was too, Dad."

The Red Cross gets involved and my departure is pushed up to the winfly flight on Sept 1. My brother will be flown back to the states and buried before I get home. After work the guys come over. We smoke some bowls, go to mid-rats and play ping pong for the millionth time this month. No one has to remind me that I'm the shortest man at McMurdo.

8/22. Word spreads around the base and a few people who wouldn't normally give me the time of night express their sympathies. A big gnarly equipment operator named Marvin Stewart shakes my hand and tells me I should be proud of my brother. I forgive the Seabees for any issues we may have had in the past.

I'm left with the image of curling black smoke rising into a sky of August blue. The Chinook is a cigar butt crushed out on a German wheat field. What would it be like to die in the company of thirty five GI's?

No one actually asks about my brother. I'm left to daydream about a helicopter explosion. Did Artie die from smoke, fire or fall? What would he look like in the morgue? I know my Dad will insist on viewing his remains. Losing his first born son- he's not going to take anyone's word for it. I'm helpless to help my Dad.

8/23. Now that I'm leaving Sept 1, I'm being looked at like a freak. Chambers says something about luck. I hope he means bad luck. Homer doesn't want to make the days seem even longer so he assigns tasks to keep me busy. We're running a firehouse. Although no one asks I'm prepared to explain my brother. He's left-handed, never got a grade less than an A and reads U.S. News and World Report cover to cover. Maybe I'm nuts but I feel like people are avoiding me - as if they might catch a case of my misfortune.

8/24. I get out of my rack after not sleeping. I want to go home and see Mom. This week is set to unfold, slow as a daytime drama on a muted TV. I have nothing else to do but consider my circumstances.

Our nightly ritual remains unchanged. Get ice for the pipe, put a foot stool behind the door to act as trip wire, clean the bowl and slice hash off the bar like a pencil shaving. Our heads are spinning until mid-rats. There's no more talk of ChiChi, renting a house and partying until they send SP's. Cheese Filled Buns is not funny anymore. Carl Dish isn't funny anymore. The Debauched Hopsodar is not funny anymore. Cynthia Meyers is not sexy anymore, Tapeman sucks. WASA is no fun. Masturbation is off the menu.

8/25. The only thing that kills time is playing ping pong. Stupid as it sounds the amount of concentration I put into beating Fang actually makes me forget everything. In the moment of reacting to his trick serve I'm away from the ice and the news of my brother's death. I never win when I play John and I don't want to win now. I'd suspect him of going easy on me. He and a guy named Paul are table tennis gunslingers at 155. There is nothing else to add to my daily recap page.

Keeping my diary grounds me. Meher Baba advises we consider a minute an hour and every hour independent as a book on a bookshelf. I'm paraphrasing but a Zen of detachment allows us to make sorrow a joy.

8/26. I do a two hour field day. Mike comes over and we work on the cruise book. Everyone is trying to keep me in the moment. Today is probably the day my brother is being buried.

8/27. Conrad helps me make a grave marker at the wood shop. I paint it with the only available paint left - a greenish grey that's been here since Scott. I spend the evening at the message center polishing up an interview I did with Charlie Webb.

8/28. Russ Peterman brings the USARP pick up to the firehouse and we load the cross on board. At this time of year you get six hours of daylight. We race out on to the ice shelf, Fang and I riding in the back of the truck, sunk down inside our parkas. When we stop for Fang and Mike to switch places, I get out and skitch on the tailgate in a standing position. Russ goes fast enough that the ice speeds under my boots like film rewinding. I am in a white fast forward. We visit Shackleton's hut at Cape Royale then on to Cape Evans where I plant the cross with my brother's name on one side. On the opposite side I have listed, Mike, Fang, Russ and Pete- under the heading Hacker's Tour and the date. Back at base, I have to get ready to go. I get a haircut because I no longer give a shit about my hair.

8/29.   SSS Interview with Charlie Webb

Charlie Webb is a first class good ole boy. Honest, uncomplicated and effective at his job – no wonder no one likes him. Charlie was Class President at Ritta Elementary School in a Tennessee town so small he didn't think it worth mentioning. He was Captain of the football and basketball team even though you can eat cake off his head.

In 1953 Charlie went Army. He was doing basic at Fort McClellan, Alabama when the Army caught on that he was only 17. At 18 he made an inter-service transfer to the Marine Corp. He came aboard at Parris Island. His boot camp troop started at 76-only 37 graduated. I ask him, "If boot camp training is any good why do we lose so many marines."

CW: We were trained to kill, not to avoid being killed. I could kill a man like stepping on a bug. Some guys killed other men right there on base."

SSS: Whoa, Charlie- we have no bugs down here.

From Parris Island Charlie landed in Korea on the day the Armistice was signed. (Good timing Jarhead!). Back at Camp Le Juene, he piped aboard the APA 36 USS. Chilton. As a BAR Rifleman Charlie spent 13 months rehearsing beach assaults. From there he was flung out into the fleet; serving on everything from a carrier to a minesweeper.

Back home as a civilian he went to work for the Kays Ice Cream company. When his daughter was diagnosed with a heart condition, Charlie joined the Navy to get medical coverage.

SSS: Did you ever see a uniform you didn't like?

CW: Even as a paper boy, I wore the company windbreaker.

The Seabees took him from Davisville to Port Hueneme and then off to Nam. His unit was building Red Beach Camp outside Da Nang.

"They gave us air mattresses and blankets to use till the barracks were up."

SSS: How were things run while you were in Nam?

CW: The same stupid resistance from officers to accept the advice of NCOs that you see at most commands. There is a widespread suspicion that enlisted men put their own interests above the mission. It's not always the case. I was Sergeant of the Guard – rules apply to everyone. That pissed off some officers - look at my quarterly marks.

On his second tour to Nam Charlie ran the UT shop at Camp Hoover. Back at Hueneme he was Chief Master at Arms at the galley. He remembers seeing Chief Tom working there.

SSS: Did you have to align the condiments?

CW: That sounds dirty.

Charlie had a cup of coffee at Davisville before arriving at McMurdo.

SSS: Tell the readers how you met your wife.

CW: I was cracking heads in a high school basketball game and she came down to the floor to chew me out. She was pretty and one of the few girls I was taller than. Five years later we were married, we have two boys and two girls.

SSS: And the heart problem?

CW: She's fine. The Navy has taken great care of her. Thanks for asking.

SSS: What about down here Charlie, what's your opinion of this mission?

CW: First of all, why? For twenty years, we've been told that we could discover things that would benefit mankind by supporting science down here. That sounds like "If the Russians are here we have to be here." Why would Russia want to rule Antarctica? Siberia's not cold enough?

SSS: Very radical, Charlie.

CW: I'm not trying to knock people. If you don't read the lines you're not going to read between them. Another thing that needs to change down here, we throw away too much stuff. When I was Master at Arms, I rescued five floor buffers from the scrap heap. They work better than ever. Each one might cost 300 dollars or more new. Chief Condon said he'd never seen such improvement in any shop. I don't think he said it because he wanted something.

SSS: Are you sure?

CW: People speak of the "command" in faraway terms. We are the command. Guys will say "The Navy sucks, fuck the Navy." Well I'm the Navy and we're not going to suck while I'm on the team.

SSS: Is there a motto that you live by?

CW: Never go anywhere you can't live.

SSS: Pretty ironic Chuck. What do you think about gun control?

CW: I own guns. I don't believe in giving them up to the government. Ask the Indians how that worked for them.

SSS: What rewards have you got from the navy?

CW: Pay. I got paid for living off base at D'ville, plus $750 a month and a $1300 re-up bonus. I'm making more money than anyone in my shop. That means a lot to a kid who didn't have a floor in his house. All my civilian life I've worked two jobs. I got my first four college credits on the ice through the PACE program. No one pushed me to get in – if you don't look around you'll leave here knowing less than you did when you came ashore.

SSS: You didn't have a floor in your house? It must have been easy to go downstairs.

CW: It sounds like I'm speaking against blind obedience and I guess I am. Young people don't accept things as they once did. If you're waging a war and expect me to pitch in, you better start by explaining why.

SSS: Well Charlie you've given us a lot to chew on. (insert chew joke). Do you want to give a thumbs-up to any of your mates?

CW: Cruz Antiporta because he's older than most people down here and does the work of a man half his age. I've seen him haul heavy gear while working outdoors and never complain. He doesn't use his age as an excuse to get out of work.

SSS: Well done Charlie. You're a hacker.

8/29. Stick, Andy, Phil, Howie, Mike and John meet at my room and smoke what's left of the hash and take the last of mescaline. I already feel high thinking I'm leaving in 48 hours but I smoke anyway. It's my going away party but no one calls it that.

8/31 I'm in bed awake. I get up and help Ed paint the number 3 truck. In the afternoon Fang and Mike do a slide show of pictures for use in our cruise book. No sense trying to sleep we play ping pong till 0400

9/1. I'm asleep when Homer shakes me to ask "Do you feel like going home?" At the disbursement desk, DK2 McCarthy issues me a pile of money. McCracken and I sit in the firehouse waiting for word that the plane has landed. I take a quick run through the 155 lunch crowd saying "Goodbyes". Commander Maddox shakes my hand and wishes me luck. Before I get on the shuttle to Willie Field, I see Fang. He's the last guy I talk to at McMurdo.

9/4. I arrive in New York after three days of military plane-hopping that ends with an American Airlines flight out of Dallas. Stepping out of the terminal with a sea bag on my shoulder, I see a woman who looks like my Mom if my Mom dyed her hair grey. The woman is running toward me. I've never seen my Mother run.

I'm in the backseat of the car with my little brother John. Dad is crying so hard he has to pull over. I'm happy to be back and pissed off. Vietnam has ruined my homecoming. My brothers and I lucked out of the war until a uniform knocked on the door. Artie is a name not on the wall.